The Sinister Omen

The high-winged seaplane performed like a dream, humming smoothly. The controls proved sensitive and responsive to Nancy's touch. But suddenly, just off the coast of South Carolina, the plane began to stutter and spit. Nancy's heart skipped a beat as she felt the craft buck.

"What's wrong?" George asked.

Nancy stared hard at the instrument panel. "The gauge isn't working! We've run out of gas!"

They were dropping fast toward the three-foot swells—the waves and whitecaps were growing larger and larger. Nancy knew that if she didn't guide the plane onto the water, they would cartwheel out of control.

Baroom! The first wave slapped the pontoons like a cannon shot. The plane reeled and bounced into the air. . . .

Nancy Drew
Mystery Stories

Available from MINSTREL Books

67

NANCY® DREW

THE SINISTER OMEN

CAROLYN KEENE

A MINSTREL® BOOK

PUBLISHED BY POCKET BOOKS

New York   London   Toronto   Sydney   Tokyo   Singapore

A Minstrel Book published by
POCKET BOOKS, a division of Simon & Schuster
1230 Avenue of the Americas, New York, NY 10020

ISBN: 0-671-73938-7

First Minstrel Books printing April 1988

10 9 8 7 6 5 4 3 2

Contents

THE SINISTER
OMEN

1

The Great, Black Buzzard

Crash!

The home of Bess Marvin, still covered by the predawn darkness, was suddenly disturbed by the sound of something falling to the floor.

"Wha—? Gerv? Uh—" came the sleepy and confused voice of Bess as she struggled to get out from under her blankets to snap on the light.

"Nancy!" she cried out a moment later.

"What's the matter?" a second sleepy voice asked from the top of the double bunk bed. It was Bess's cousin, George Fayne, whose face now appeared over the side, eyes blinking and dark hair tousled.

"It's Nancy," said Bess. "Look at her. She's fallen out of bed!"

She pointed to her disheveled friend in pale blue pajamas who was curled up on the floor across the room. Nancy was moving her legs in a running motion as she groaned and made little cries of distress.

"She's having a nightmare!" George declared. "Wake her up, Bess."

"Me?" Bess cried, brushing her blond hair back from her face, her blue eyes growing wide with alarm. "Oh, no. I read somewhere that if you wake up somebody having a nightmare their heart might stop. Or they go into shock or something."

"Oh, Bess!" George looked at her relative with some exasperation. "Nancy's very healthy and she doesn't have heart problems. So you can wake her up."

Bess hesitated. "I'd feel better if you did it."

George climbed down and knelt beside Nancy. She took her friend's face gently in her hands. "Come on, Nancy," she said. "It was just a dream. Wake up!"

Gingerly, Bess came over and knelt next to the two. She rubbed Nancy's hands until at last the girl opened her large, blue eyes. At first, they were still filled with fright, but Nancy quickly relaxed once she saw that she was safely in Bess's bedroom with her friends.

"Oh, where did it go?" she moaned.

"Where did what go?" Bess asked. "It was a nightmare, Nancy, a bad dream. But you're okay now."

"Oh-h-h." Nancy shuddered. "It was awful. Awful. I never get nightmares. Why should I get one now?"

"Too much pepperoni pizza last night." George laughed.

"And too much pistachio ice cream with hot fudge and whipped cream," Bess added.

"If that's so," Nancy said, "how come *you* two didn't have nightmares?"

"We're used to junk food," George replied with a chuckle.

"Tell us about your dream," Bess urged. "I'm dying to know what happened!"

"Hm," Nancy said, feeling strong enough to get up and sit down on the edge of her bed. "Let me try and remember. It had something to do with our going to Fort Lauderdale to meet Dad and chase the stamp smugglers and all that."

"What stamp smugglers?" Bess demanded, looking apprehensive. "Don't tell me you're going to become involved in another mystery while we're in the middle of our spring vacation?"

"Well—" Nancy grinned. "It's really Dad

who's involved in the mystery this time."

"You mean your father's in Florida trying to catch a bunch of stamp smugglers?" Bess asked.

"Right. He's working with his long-time friend and client, Señor Ricardo Segovia, on a case."

"The same Señor Segovia who invited us to stay in his house?" George inquired.

"Yes."

"That figures," Bess complained. "She tells us all about her father's wealthy friend who wants us to stay in his twenty-two room mansion for our spring vacation, but she never mentions that our host and Mr. Drew are working on a mystery!"

"And we don't believe for one minute that you won't help, Nancy!" George added. "And that means we'll be caught up in it, too."

"And here I thought we'd just have a good time!" Bess grumbled.

"We will," Nancy said placatingly. "You see, Señor Segovia often does undercover and consulting work for the U.S. government. At present, he's tracking down a network of international crooks who specialize in stealing and smuggling rare stamps. Now, he didn't *ask* me to help him, but if there's something I can do—"

"Of course," George said.

"Doesn't the case intrigue you?"

Bess looked skeptical. "I'll tell you when it's all over. But you seem so intrigued that you're having nightmares."

"Oh, yes," Nancy said. "The nightmare."

"I know." George grinned. "You dreamed you were being chased by an Emerson College senior in a gorilla suit."

"Be serious," Bess begged. "I want to hear."

"Well," Nancy began, "I imagined that I was in Fort Lauderdale and I was being chased, you're right about that. It was night, and I was followed by cars, boats, and helicopters. They even had guard dogs after me."

"They?" Bess asked.

"Well, in nightmares you never seem to recognize who it is that you're afraid of. The only thing I can remember is a great, black, shadowy outline of something. A bird. A bird of prey. No, that's not right. A bird that eats carrion, dead bodies. A vulture or a buzzard or something like that."

"Ecch." Bess shuddered.

"Oh, I don't know," George quipped. "It could have been worse. It could have been an Emerson College senior in a gorilla suit."

All three girls broke up laughing. Then Bess

5

said, "I'm sorry, Nancy. It must have been horrible, but it's over now and you woke up and we didn't give you a heart attack so let's all go back to bed and get some sleep. We have a long trip ahead of us in the morning."

"Right," Nancy agreed. "Everybody back to bed and my apologies for my vulture or whatever it was."

The girls were just getting settled under the covers again, when they heard an auto horn honking under their bedroom window.

"Oh, it couldn't be," George cried out. "It's the middle of the night!"

"No, it isn't," Nancy said. "It's five o'clock!"

The horn honked again. Bess chuckled. "It's them, all right. It's the boys."

Nancy and George had stayed at Bess's house overnight in order to get an early start to Florida the next morning. The "boys" they referred to were three Emerson College seniors, Ned Nickerson, Dave Evans, and Burt Eddleton. They were driving to Fort Lauderdale in Ned's father's Land Rover, assuming the girls were making the trip in Nancy's blue sports sedan.

The girls popped their heads out the window and saw the three young men smiling and waving at them.

Ned, who had long had a fondness for Nancy,

stood up tall in the front passenger seat. His dark eyes were teasing as he called, "Don't tell me you're still in bed. We're going to be south of Washington, D.C., before you even get started."

Burt, who was driving, called to George. "You want me to save you a shady space under a beach umbrella? It's going to be awfully crowded in Fort Lauderdale by the time you get there."

The girls hooted back at their friends, a bit weakly because they were still half asleep.

"Never mind, Bess," called Dave Evans, a rangy, blond boy with green eyes who lounged in the back seat, making a bed of the duffle bags stuffed with the boys' possessions. "You'll probably show up by the middle of next week. I mean, half a week's vacation is better than none."

At that point, the front door of the house opened and Mrs. Marvin cried out, "Boys, boys, you should know better than to make such a commotion at this hour of the morning. You'll wake up all the neighbors!"

Ned and his friends promptly quieted down, looking a little abashed. "We're sorry, Mrs. Marvin," Ned apologized.

7

Mrs. Marvin, who could never be stern for too long, smiled. "All right. Now get going. And here, I made you some sandwiches and cookies. You'll just have to pick up milk or soft drinks along the way."

Thanking her, the boys took the food, called out quiet good-byes to the girls, and pulled away with a minimum of engine roar.

"Oh, dear," George said, hugging a pillow and flopping on Bess's bunk. "Oh, dear, the poor dears. They don't know."

Nancy laughed. "No, they don't know we're going by plane and we're going to beat them by two full days."

"Yet," Bess said, a worried look creasing her pretty face, "I feel kind of mean, doing that to the boys."

"Mean?" George challenged. "Didn't you just hear them gloating about getting there first? Don't you think it would be good for their souls and make them more modest and humble if we three girls arrived ahead of them?"

Bess giggled. "I suppose so."

The three girls dressed and went down to breakfast. They had packed the night before and were ready to leave as soon as they had finished eating. After fond good-byes and hugs

8

and kisses from Mrs. Marvin, they piled into Nancy's car and were on their way to the airport. But they had not even driven a dozen blocks when Nancy said very quietly, "Don't look back. Don't do anything. But there's a car following us!"

2

Sabotage!

"I hate this," Bess said. "Whenever a car follows us I know what it means. It means Nancy is going on another case, even if we don't know what it is yet."

"Don't be a pessimist," George told her. "Maybe it's somebody going to the airport, too."

"Not likely," Nancy declared, her blue eyes flashing to the rearview mirror and back to the road. "I've tested him out by slowing down and giving him a chance to pass us. He didn't take it. He's just hanging in there behind us."

"Can you see who it is?" George asked.

"No. It's a small, green sports car with one of those tinted glass windshields; the kind where you can't see in very well but you can see out."

"What are you going to do?" Bess asked.

"I don't know," Nancy replied. "I don't know whether just to ignore him or try to lose him."

"Let's lose him," George suggested. "But how?"

"Oh, we can do a few tricks that won't break the law," the titian-haired sleuth responded. With that, she pulled up and stopped. The move took the green car by surprise. Before the driver could react, he found that with another car directly behind him, he had no choice but to pass the girls. As soon as he did, Nancy made a smooth U-turn, went back over the brow of a hill until she was sure the green car was out of sight, then turned right onto an alternate road to the airport.

"That did it," George said. "It's so easy when you know how."

But five miles farther on, Nancy looked into her mirror and groaned. "It's so easy, is it? He's back again."

This time the two girls whirled around and saw the green sports car a hundred yards behind.

"Well," Nancy said, "let's not worry about it. He's not bothering us and we're going to a crowded airport where he's not likely to try anything."

The girls drove on for another ten minutes.

11

Then Bess, who couldn't resist looking back furtively, cleared her throat. "Ah, Nancy?"

"Yes?"

"If I tell you something, will you promise not to take your hands off the wheel and scream?"

"Nancy Drew has never taken her hands off the wheel and screamed in her entire life," George stated.

"Okay. Now there are *two* cars following us. The green one and right behind it a yellow station wagon."

"I know," Nancy said. "I just didn't say anything because I didn't want to upset you. We might have a whole parade before we get to the airport."

She tried to think of a reason why people would be trailing her. Could it have anything to do with the legal actions her father was undertaking on behalf of Señor Segovia in Florida?

Before she could reach any conclusion on the matter, they had arrived at River Heights Airport. Nancy drove straight to the charter plane area and parked. The girls got out and looked around for their "shadows." They didn't see the green car, but the yellow station wagon pulled in next to them. To their surprise, the driver, who got out and approached the trio, was a woman.

"This is it," Bess whispered. "Here comes trouble, Detective Drew. I can feel it."

The woman had pleasant features and earnest brown eyes. Her dark blond hair was tied back tightly and she wore glasses with large, clear plastic rims.

"Nancy Drew?" she asked, stopping a few feet from the girls. Then, not waiting for Nancy to reply, she said, "Oh, excuse me. Let me introduce myself first. I'm Susan McAfee? From Fort Lauderdale?" She had the habit of many Southerners of ending a statement with a rising intonation to make it sound like a question.

"Oh, hi," Nancy said. "Yes, I'm Nancy Drew. And these are my friends, Bess Marvin and George Fayne."

"Miss Drew, I don't want to delay you. I know you're trying to get to Fort Lauderdale and . . ."

Nancy started. "How did you know?"

"Well," Miss McAfee replied, "I know your father, Carson Drew. He's an old friend of my employer, Mrs. Eleanor Palmer. May I speak to you privately and explain?"

Nancy put her arms around Bess and George. "You can say anything you want in the presence of Bess and George. They're my dearest friends and confidantes."

"Oh, all right." Miss McAfee smiled. "But could we at least go inside and have sodas while I tell you my problem? I'm awfully thirsty."

Nancy agreed and the four young women went inside and settled down in a comfortable booth in the restaurant. Then Susan McAfee took a deep breath and began.

"I am the personal secretary and companion to Mrs. Eleanor Palmer. Mrs. Palmer is very wealthy. And very courageous. And extremely opinionated. She is also bright and funny and sharp as a tack. And she is ninety-three years old, mind you."

"Wow," said Nancy, "she must be quite a lady."

"She is. I hope you get to meet her because you'll find it quite an experience. Anyway, Mrs. Palmer, as I said, is an old friend of your family. She knew your father's grandparents quite well."

"They weren't alive any more when I was born," Nancy said.

Miss McAfee nodded and went on. "Mrs. Palmer has an annoying and unusual problem. It's a little scary, really. She and I and her servants live in a huge, old house. Everything is done in the Victorian style of the 1890s. Great, massive furniture, heavy mauve drapes. It's a little like living in a museum."

"But not scary, is it?" Bess put in.

"No. But what has happened is. Mrs. Palmer is plagued by burglars. Only they don't steel anything!"

"I beg your pardon," Nancy said, looking quizzically at the young woman.

"That's right," Miss McAfee replied. "They don't take anything. They break into the house and ransack it, but in the end nothing's missing."

"Could they just be vandals?" George asked. "Perhaps neighborhood children who think it's fun to destroy things?"

"No," Miss McAfee said. "These people are professionals. There is no doubt of that. Our security precautions would keep out any amateur thieves or vandals."

"How many times has it happened?" Nancy asked.

"Four times. Isn't that unbelievable? I must tell you that Mrs. Palmer has given the Fort Lauderdale Police a very hard time. She has also complained to the Broward County Sheriff's Office and the Florida State Highway Patrol."

"Is there special protection now?" Nancy

asked with concern. "At her home, I mean?"

"Yes. The police have a man on guard. But if there's another burglary, I think Mrs. Palmer will try to have the entire city and county government replaced."

The girls laughed. "A feisty old lady," Nancy said.

Susan McAfee nodded. "Sometimes she does try your patience, but she has so much character and spunk that you have to admire her."

Nancy agreed. "Well, Miss McAfee, what do you intend to do about this problem?"

"I think you know. Mrs. Palmer sent me to ask you if you will take the case while you're in Fort Lauderdale."

Bess cast her eyes heavenward and touched Nancy's foot under the table. Nancy ignored her, though she smiled a little.

"Why did you fly all the way up here when you knew I was coming to Florida?" she asked Susan.

"Mrs. Palmer wants her answers right away."

Nancy laughed. "I know, but she could have telephoned."

"That's something else. She doesn't trust telephones. She doesn't really trust anything invented in the last one hundred years."

Nancy drummed her fingers on the table.

16

"Miss McAfee, I'd like to help but we were going to be on vacation and . . ."

"Mrs. Palmer said she would more than match any price you might want to set."

Nancy shook her head. "We never take money. That's not the issue."

There was silence. Then Bess spoke. "Well, Mrs. Palmer is so old. And she is a friend of your family so it probably wouldn't be polite to say no, would it? I mean, I don't want to make your decisions for you, Nancy, but . . ."

Nancy and George were both amused. "Well," George said. "Look who's becoming an agent for Nancy Drew, detective. I thought you wanted to vacation with us!"

Bess grinned ruefully. "We'll work it in. We have to help Mrs. Palmer!"

3

Air-Sea Rescue

Nancy extended her hand to Susan McAfee. "My most tenderhearted friend Bess has been my conscience," she said. "Tell Mrs. Palmer we'll take the case."

Susan heaved a sigh and shook Nancy's hand. "You don't know what a relief this is. I've been rehearsing in my mind what a tongue-lashing I'd get if I went home and told her you didn't want to do it."

Nancy smiled and took down the address and phone number. She noted that even though Mrs. Palmer distrusted telephones, she had given in to Susan and had one installed. Then the girls parted from the young woman and made their way to the area where a beautiful, white, high-winged seaplane rolled gently in the Muskoka River alongside a small dock. It was the craft that Carson Drew had chartered as a present for his daughter and her friends. There was plenty of room for all three girls and their luggage.

An attendant loaded the bags and asked the trio if they had brought lunch.

"Oh, dear!" Bess wailed. "Mother made us terrific sandwiches to take along, but we got so busy saying good-bye that we forgot them!"

"Don't worry," the attendant said. "You get whole meals right over there, packed to take along on airplanes. When you're ready to go, just pick up something."

He handed Nancy the ignition key. "It's all gassed and checked out. Did you file your flight plan?"

"Not yet," Nancy replied. "But I'll do that while my friends get the lunch."

The girls separated. Nancy went into the office to clear the flight. When she came out and was walking toward the dock again, a man in mechanic's overalls came toward her. He had a cap pulled low over his face, and, after a quick glance at the girl, he turned his head away.

When he had passed her, Nancy stared after him. He certainly acted strange, she thought. I wonder who he—

"Nancy!" came Bess's voice. "Come on, we're ready to leave!"

Nancy waved and ran up to the dock, forgetting about the unfriendly mechanic.

"I hope you brought your pilot's license," George said as she climbed into the copilot's seat.

Nancy grinned. "I did, but I'm not used to flying a seaplane. Once we're up in the air, I might not get us down again!"

Bess spread herself luxuriously in the double back seat. "Then I suppose we'll be flying forever. As long as the weather's this beautiful, I won't mind."

The engine started without a hitch and the shiny white plane leaped forward over the water. It gained speed, shuddering slightly as it skipped along. Bess gripped the back of Nancy's seat.

"What's happening?" she asked tensely, trying not to let her voice tremble. "It feels like the thing is falling apart."

"It's not!" Nancy shouted over the engine roar. "This is the normal way a seaplane takes off." She eased back the stick, and the plane gracefully lifted off the water and began to climb.

"Thank goodness." Bess sighed.

It was a clear, sunny day, and with George serving as navigator, holding the maps on her lap, they flew down the eastern seaboard. They passed New York City with its tall buildings, and saw the figure of the Statue of Liberty, on Liberty Island in the harbor.

They continued along the New Jersey coast past Atlantic City and the long, slender spit of Cape May. After they swung out to sea to go around the restricted area of the great naval station at Norfolk, Virginia, they broke out the lunches they had bought at the airport.

The engine's roar didn't encourage conversation but the girls were feeling so exuberant that they began shouting back and forth to one another anyway, in between bites of luscious sandwiches filled with roast beef, Swiss cheese, salami, and tuna salad.

"That's Cape Hatteras," Nancy shouted, pointing down to her right. "Very bumpy down there if you're in a ship."

"Why?" Bess shouted back.

"I don't know. Something to do with the way the Gulf Stream comes up the coast and then veers off east. Anyway, it's always rough. And when they have storms, it's worse than anywhere else. Do you know what they call it?"

"What!" George yelled.

"The Graveyard of Ships."

Both Bess and George went through the pantomime of shuddering.

The plane performed like a dream, humming smoothly. The controls proved sensitive and responsive to Nancy's touch. The easy drone of the engine at last had its effect on Bess. With a full stomach, she fell asleep.

Suddenly, just off the coast of South Carolina, the plane began to stutter and spit. Nancy's heart skipped a beat as she felt the craft buck slightly.

"What's wrong?" George asked.

"I don't know," Nancy replied as she worked frantically to nurse the engine back to a normal rhythm. "It doesn't make sense."

"Do you have enough gas?"

"Yes. I have a full tank—" Nancy stared hard at the panel. "Wait a minute. That can't be right. We've only covered half the flight. The gauge isn't working! I think we've run out of gas!"

"What are we going to do?" George called, beginning to turn pale.

Without replying, Nancy switched to the radio channel she knew would give her communications with nearby stations. "Charleston Tower, this is November four seven six five two. Mayday! Mayday! We're about five miles west of Charleston Harbor. I have no power and must land. Can you guide me? Over."

There was silence and then a voice crackled over the receiver. "November four seven six five two, we have you on radar. Are you amphibious? Over."

"No, this is a seaplane," Nancy replied. "A pontoon aircraft. Can you help me? Over."

"How does the sea look to you? Over."

"Choppy. Over."

"We don't think you have any choice. Can you come down close to the island you see on your right? Over."

"I'll try. Please alert air-sea rescue. Over."

"Air-sea rescue has been alerted. You'll be all right. Remember to keep your nose up on landing. Good luck. Over."

Nancy glanced at George and found her friend doing her best to keep calm. She even tried a smile. Nancy patted her hand.

"We're going to make it. Don't worry."

"I don't doubt it. But I hope Bess stays asleep until we land. If she wakes up and starts carrying on, I'm going to sit on her!"

Nancy's face was tense since by now the engine had stopped altogether.

"Here we go!" she said. "Get into your life jacket, and then help Bess with hers. And start praying!"

4

Nightmare Come True?

"Oh, please let's not wake Bess up!" George objected, struggling with her life vest.

"If we have to swim for it, you don't want her to drown, do you?" Nancy challenged, as she kept the nose of the plane down slightly to insure they could continue to glide and not stall out.

"No," George said, and turned toward the back seat. "Bess, Bess, wake up!"

"Ummmm. Are we there yet?"

"Well, we're not exactly there but you'll have to put on your jacket because we're landing."

"Oh," Bess said. "Where?"

"By that island down there."

"Okay." Then, suddenly, Bess sat bolt upright. "Wait a minute. What happened to the engine?"

"It stalled out. But it's going to be all right. Now put that life jacket on, hurry!"

Bess quickly slipped into the vest. "I'm ready," she said weakly.

"Good girl," George said.

Nancy only half heard them, for she was concentrating very hard on the controls in front of her. Keeping the stick slightly forward, she saw the ocean coming nearer. She flicked her eyes back and forth to the altimeter that indicated how high they were. She had been watching the needle move slowly from five thousand feet to forty-five hundred to four thousand and on downward.

George had her hands braced against the instrument panel in front of her. As she saw the waves and whitecaps becoming larger and larger, she had to bite her lip to keep from calling out, "Pull up, Nancy!" But she knew the girl had to move the stick back at precisely the right moment, or all would be lost.

If she did it too soon, the plane would stall and spin out or, at best, pancake flat and heavily into the ocean. If she pulled it back too late, the nose and pontoon tips would go in and they would probably cartwheel over the waves. Either way, it would be dangerous and frightening.

The ideal way was to bring the plane in level with the waves, riding just a few feet above them, then gradually let the pontoons settle in.

With the altimeter reading 100 feet, Nancy began easing back. Not fast enough! Hastily, she yanked on the stick and the nose came up barely in time to miss the waves. The plane leveled off and then began dropping toward the three foot swells.

Baroom! The first wave slapped the pontoons like a cannon shot, causing a cry from Bess. The plane reeled, bounced into the air, glided a bit further, and came down again with another *Barooom!* But with no bounce. This time they were bobbing on the ocean's surface like a pretty, white cork.

"Oh, no," Bess called from the rear, struggling out from under a suitcase that had broken open and dumped clothes all over the seat. "Are we dead?"

"No," Nancy said cheerily, "we're in South Carolina." Suddenly, she started as a face appeared outside her window. Then her surprise turned to a squeal of delight. "Mr. Blaine!"

"Who?" said George.

"Mr. Blaine. Fred Blaine. You know, the newsman from television? He's here in a little boat!"

She opened the door and Fred Blaine peered in. He was gray-haired and distinguished-looking, with piercing but kindly blue eyes. "Nancy Drew! We never know when you'll be dropping in, do we?"

"Mr. Blaine! What on earth are you doing here?"

"Me? I live here. You've just landed in my front yard. I own this land right along the beach. That's my house over there. Didn't you know?"

"Oh . . . I didn't when I was coming down to land but now I remember Dad telling me you had built a new home here. Oh, what luck this is!"

Fred Blaine had retired a year before from his job as a network newscaster. But as a veteran navy pilot and a lifelong lover of boats and the ocean, it was natural that he should make his home on an island close to the sea, where he kept a forty-foot sailboat and a motorboat. The Charleston Tower had contacted him when Nancy was going to land in the area, and he had been ready the moment she made her approach.

As Fred Blaine helped the girls into his boat so they could go ashore, one of his two teenage sons, Robert, took charge of the plane. He towed it into the protected area of the Blaine dock.

"I want to congratulate you, Nancy," Mr. Blaine said. "That was one of the finest dead-stick landings I've ever seen."

"It was?" Nancy was pleased but unbelieving. "It didn't feel like it from where I was sitting. I thought I almost tore the poor plane apart."

"No, no." Mr. Blaine laughed. "One bump and you were in. Anyway, you know what they used to tell aviation cadets when they were training. Any landing is a good landing if you can walk away from it."

"Or, in our case," said George, "if you can float away from it."

"Right."

Mr. Blaine chuckled. "Your pilot was cool all the way. But speaking of cool, it's terribly hot today. Let's go up to the house where Mrs. Blaine is waiting for us."

Linda Blaine was an attractive, motherly woman with her long, gray hair done in an elaborately plaited bun. She took the three visitors in hand, hurrying them through the house and onto the patio on the other side. There she served them cold drinks and cookies.

"I hope you'll stay overnight," she said. "We'd love to have you."

Gladly, the trio accepted the invitation. After they had refreshed themselves and notified Señor Segovia of their delay, they reclined by the pool and talked with the Blaines' two sons, Robert and Edward. They were both handsome boys with dark hair and eyes who made it obvious that they wished their pretty young guests would stay for a week.

Fred Blaine joined the group and sat down. "When you get to where you're going, Nancy," he said, "I hope you report the people who were responsible for maintaining the plane. Your gas tank was flat empty and could not have been full when you started."

"I know," Nancy said. "But I also have a hunch it was not the attendant's fault. Somebody followed us to the airport, you see." She told the story about the two cars and Susan McAfee. "Now I know why the second car was tailing us," she concluded. "And I even saw the guy who I think was responsible for draining our gas. He wore a mechanic's overall and had his cap pulled so low over his face that I couldn't recognize his features. He looked suspicious, but since I didn't see him near the plane, I didn't give it much thought."

"Do you have any idea who he could be?" Mr. Blaine asked.

Nancy explained that the culprit might be tied in with her father's work for Ricardo Segovia in Fort Lauderdale.

Mr. Blaine stared at her in surprise. "You mean the business with the smuggled stamps?"

"Yes."

"Hm, that could be. You know, I had my collection stolen about two months ago. It wasn't all that valuable, but I had a few rather rare stamps. The insurance paid the loss, of course. But it can't make up for something that's been important to me."

Nancy expressed her sympathy and suggested that maybe her father and Ricardo Segovia might recover the Blaine collection.

"Perhaps," Mr. Blaine said. "But, Nancy, tell me, what is the significance of that frightening drawing on the side of your plane?"

"What do you mean?"

"Well, in the military, the pilots often have artists draw cartoon characters of movie stars or something like that on their airplanes. On your plane, there is this picture of a brooding, black vulture!"

"What?" Nancy gasped, instantly remembering the creature of her nightmare.

"Yes, a vulture with its wings half spread, crouching. It's very low, almost underneath the plane, that's why you probably didn't notice it. But it's really spine chilling!"

5

The Vulture Strikes Again!

"A vulture!" Nancy repeated.

"Oh, no," Bess said. "It couldn't be. Nancy, don't even think about it."

George got up from her lounge chair and sat down anxiously next to the titian-haired detective. "It's all right, Nancy. I'm sure there's no connection."

Mr. Blaine looked confused. "What connection? What are you talking about?"

Nancy found it difficult to speak, and George, sensing this, patted her hand. "Well, it may seem silly," she said, "but last night, before we came down here, we all stayed at Bess's house. Just before dawn, Nancy had a nightmare. She said a vulture was chasing her!"

Mr. Blaine smiled. "I know how you feel. I

33

had something like that happen when I was working in television. I had a dream about being chased by a man who was dressed in black. Really terrifying. Well, a year passed and I was at a dinner where awards were to be given for journalism. I had been selected to hand out the little trophies. Suddenly, when I announced a certain name, a man got up, all dressed in black. I almost dropped the prize. He was the guy from my nightmare!"

"And you had never seen him before?" Bess gasped.

"Never. He was a reporter for a paper in Pennsylvania. A perfectly nice fellow. I knew him for many years after that and one day told him of my nightmare. We had a good laugh about it. But absolutely nothing happened. To this day, he has never chased me."

Nancy smiled at Mr. Blaine's effort to cheer her up. "I know you're right," she said. "It's silly to get upset about dreams or goblins on Halloween or any of that. But after somebody tried to make our plane crash and painted that vulture symbol on the side, I naturally feel a little funny about it."

"You know," George said, "it could just be something the owner put on the plane, and we would never have thought anything of it if it hadn't been for the man draining our gas." All agreed that that was probably true.

"Just the same," Bess said, "I'd rather not have it on the plane. I don't even want to see it."

"I do," George declared, getting up.

"So do I," Nancy added.

"We'll take you," Robert volunteered. "You see, we noticed the drawing when we gassed up your plane. At the time, we didn't think anything of it."

The girls thanked the boys and followed them to the dock, where the boats and their seaplane were moored.

When they saw the vulture symbol, Nancy's heart beat faster again. It looked so much like the one in her dream!

"Does it come off?" she asked.

Ed began to scrape at it with his fingernail. "It's a decal," he declared. "Once we get the edges loose, it'll peel easily."

In a few minutes, the offending image was gone. Nancy tried hard to put it out of her mind when the four young people returned to the Blaine house, where they spent a pleasant evening playing cards until bedtime.

The next morning, they were up early and ready to leave by nine o'clock. The Blaine family took them to the dock and saw them off.

"How about stopping by on your return trip east?" Ed called out, giving George a longing look.

"Oh, I-I'd love to," she said, waving good-bye.

"We'll take you sailing!" Robert promised, blowing a kiss to Nancy.

She smiled as the white plane lifted off smoothly. Blessed with another beautiful day, they enjoyed more panoramic views of the coastline as they passed Savannah, Jacksonville, and the famous rocket launching site at Cape Canaveral, which reminded Nancy of another adventure the girls had had there. At the time, Bess and George had been involved in a car accident and Bess had narrowly escaped being nipped by an alligator.

They laughed about it as they recalled those days, but all agreed they would prefer not to go through it again.

Within a few hours, Nancy pointed ahead and announced, "There it is, friends. Fort Lauderdale! The Venice of America!"

"Wow," Bess said, "look at all those canals!"

The girls were breathless at the sight of the lovely city with the Intracoastal Waterway slashing through it from north to south. Hundreds of interlaced canals gave almost everyone a backyard with a water route to the sea. Farther to the west, the girls could see the vast space of the famous "River of Grass" called the Everglades. Containing swamps, mangroves, high swamp grass, and few forests of hardwoods and pines, it had received its name because, from the air, only the luscious vegetation could be seen. The fact was hidden that the Everglades for much of the year was an enormously wide river sweeping out of central Florida and emptying into the Gulf of Mexico.

Nancy descended in a gentle circle as they passed directly over the Fort Lauderdale public beach. The three-mile-long strip was already beginning to fill up with thousands of students on spring break, and the roads leading into town were jammed with cars bringing still more young people to the vacation Mecca.

Nancy landed the plane with just a few skips in the water next to the public seaplane dock. As they tied up and climbed out, they were met by a uniformed chauffeur, a tall, sad-eyed man with an olive complexion. He smiled and tried to appear cheerful but Nancy could see that he was troubled by something.

"Miss Drew?" he asked politely. "May I ask which of you ladies is Miss Nancy Drew?"

Nancy identified herself and the chauffeur bowed from the waist. "We are so happy to welcome all of you to Fort Lauderdale. I'm André, chauffeur to Señor Ricardo Segovia. If you will be good enough to come with me, you and your friends, I'll drive you to the mansion."

Nancy thanked him as he led them to a beautiful gray limousine that seemed as long as a football field. He seated them and then went back for their luggage, reappearing in a few minutes with his arms full. After stowing it away in the trunk, he got into the driver's seat and then paused before putting the car into motion.

"Miss Drew," he said hesitantly, "I must tell you something, and I want to do it in a manner that will not alarm you. Since Señor Segovia could not be here, he authorized me to—"

His sentence was drowned out by a little scream from Bess. "Oh, no. Look!" She pointed to the roof of the car. There, directly above the girls' heads, was the dark, brooding picture of a vulture!

They stared at the ceiling and cringed. Neither Nancy nor George could speak. The effect on André was like that of an electric shock. He leaped from his seat, almost tore off the back door on his side, and reached in to rip away the offending decal of the evil bird.

"Oh, young ladies," he cried, "please, my apologies. It's nothing. Just a prank. A schoolboy must have slipped into the car while I was greeting you at the dock. I know it frightened you, but—" He tried to smile. "I assure you it's nothing."

Nancy and the girls exchanged looks.

"That wasn't just a prank," Bess finally declared. "Someone's after us. He stuck one of those things on our airplane, too. And he drained half our gas tank. We ran out of fuel at Charleston and had to make an emergency landing."

"She's right, André," Nancy said, now in full control of herself. "Someone *is* trying to frighten or harm us!"

André nodded. "Perhaps you are right. I—we had better go to the mansion."

He started the car and took them on a slow, safe ride to the Segovia home. The scenery was lovely but the girls barely noticed it, so upset were they by the reappearance of the grisly symbol.

"It's so evil-looking," Bess said, shuddering.

"It's like an omen," George added.

Nancy nodded. "I'm afraid it is. A sinister omen!"

6

The Sinister Omen

George frowned. "But it's not natural. It isn't something that just happens, like lightning or an earthquake. It's a man-made omen, and a threat!"

They rode in silence for a time, then Bess spoke up. "I guess that was what André wanted to talk to us about. But I screamed and interrupted him."

"That can't be," Nancy said. "If he knew the omen was there, he would have torn it down before we got in. Didn't you see the way he jumped?"

"That's right! There must be something else he's trying to tell us."

Nancy tapped on the glass panel dividing the chauffeur's compartment from the passenger section that had been closed at the start of the drive. André slid back the panel.

"Yes, Miss Drew?"

"What was it you were going to tell us?"

Nancy saw the man's hands tighten on the wheel and the color drain from his face. "I . . . I cannot tell you now. I made a mistake. It is not the proper place. I am not the proper person. Wait until we get to the mansion, please." He shut the compartment partition with a firm snap.

"Better leave him alone," George said. "He's very distressed about something."

By the time the girls arrived at the Segovia home, they were tense and worried. André helped them out and escorted them up the steps where they were met by a dignified woman of middle age identified as Consuelo, the Segovia housekeeper. She assigned a maid to the visitors and saw to it that they were taken to their private rooms. For a few moments, the opulence and grandeur of the Segovia mansion took the girls' breath away and they forgot the question of André's mysterious silence.

The chauffeur disappeared without saying anything, bringing in their luggage so quickly that before they knew it, the bags were all in the right rooms and André had vanished.

Frustrated, Nancy tried to track down Consuelo. But she, too, was nowhere to be found, having told the girls that the maid would take care of all their needs including any snacks or full meals they might wish.

"Oh-h," Nancy said, shaking her hair from side to side, "this is maddening. I know that what André had to say was terribly important. In fact, it was scaring him. I wonder where Dad or Señor Segovia are."

She decided to ask the maid, and received a smiling comment in Spanish, which she could not understand. But after much smiling back and forth and a lot of arm waving and sign language, she managed to make her question understood. And the maid gave her the answer. Her father and Señor Segovia were not here, but Nancy would see them later.

The girl thanked her, remembering the Spanish words. "*Muchas gracias,*" she said.

"You're welcome," the maid replied in English as she curtsied and left.

Nancy bathed in a huge tub with black soap, something she had never seen before, and wrapped herself in a white towel that was almost as big as a bed sheet. She then blow-dried her hair and lay on her side on a chaise longue sipping the lemonade the maid had brought.

What a life, she thought. But then she began

puzzling again about André's secret. Something was wrong. But what? Was it something about her dad? Or Señor Segovia? Or was it Mrs. Palmer? She knew she had to call Mrs. Palmer but she hesitated to get involved in that case until she was sure of what was happening with the stamp smugglers. And then, there was that buzzard symbol. The sinister omen. And her nightmare. Nancy was worried.

At five o'clock, the girls met downstairs and were thinking of a swim before dinner, when Señor Segovia arrived. He was a tall and handsome man with a dashing manner, about the same age as Carson Drew. But where the attorney was cool, methodical, and almost scientific in his approach, Señor Segovia was obviously fiery, impulsive, and a man of quick action. Nancy understood instantly why he and her father made such a good team. Each had characteristics to complement the other.

Bess and George had to suppress giggles when Señor Segovia bowed and kissed their hands upon being introduced. But after exchanging some pleasantries with the girls, their host drew Nancy aside and his face became serious.

"Nancy, I must tell you about your father."

A cold hand seemed to grip the girl's heart.

She halfway knew what was coming. It was the message André had been too afraid to deliver and that had made Consuelo hide somewhere in the house until Señor Segovia came home.

"Dad? Something has happened to Dad?"

"Nothing bad. Nothing we can't correct. He's going to be all right."

"Is he in a hospital?"

"No, no. Nothing like that. He's—well—been kidnapped. The group we've been fighting must be really terrified—and stupid—to do such a thing. They must know they can't get away with it!"

"Yes," Nancy interrupted, "but the point is my dad *was* kidnapped. We don't know where he is or how to rescue him."

"Ah," said Señor Segovia, waggling a long forefinger. "We know exactly where they have taken him and we're about to close in tonight. That's why I must ask you to excuse me again so I can help direct the search." He bowed and began to move toward the door, calling over his shoulder, "Now don't worry, Nancy. I promise you he will be all right."

"Señor Segovia!" Nancy's voice was so firm that the man turned around. "Do you really think that while my father is in danger, I'm just going to sit here and do nothing about it?"

Her host looked at her intently. Then he smiled, and motioned with one hand. "Come," he said. "I should have known better. But I think Bess and George should stay here."

George looked as if she were going to object at first, but Bess nodded silently and pulled her cousin by the hand. "It's a whole search party," she whispered. "We'd probably be more of a hindrance than a help."

Nancy and Señor Segovia left the mansion in an old, battered Volkswagen. "We must not advertise who we are or that we are coming," he said.

They drove south, out of Fort Lauderdale, past Hollywood and Miami proper, into the southwest district of the city. Their destination was a dark and deserted section, an area of warehouses in which few people traveled at night and those who did were generally considered to be up to no good.

"How do you know Dad is here?" Nancy asked.

"Through an informer," Señor Segovia replied. "Your father had not been missing for more than a day when I received a phone call telling me where he could be found."

"How do you know you can trust your source?" the girl went on.

"I have worked with this man before. He is reliable."

"Then why do you and Dad have such a hard time rounding up the men behind this stamp smuggling racket?"

"Ah," Señor Segovia replied, "that is because that gang is very clever. They deal through middlemen all the time. You never catch anyone but the underlings, and they don't even know who their bosses are. But eventually we will find out!"

As they were talking, he pointed ahead to a long, low warehouse set back from the road. "That's it," he said as they drove past. "We'll come back, of course. But I wanted you to notice the old cars parked there. See how one is run up on the sidewalk as if it had been abandoned there? Those are police cars. There are plainclothesmen inside waiting for my signal."

Nancy nodded. "Who owns the building?" she asked.

"It belongs to a firm that buys up the inventory of companies that go out of business and then resells the stuff. I understand they are not doing too well. A lot of merchandise they have acquired does not seem to be moving."

Señor Segovia drove a mile down the road, then came back with the lights out, and parked

46

a hundred yards from the building. When they got out, they left the doors slightly ajar rather than slamming them and making a warning noise. Then they walked cautiously toward the building in almost pitch darkness. Suddenly, Nancy felt someone on her left side and the hairs on her forearms stood up.

"Señor Segovia," she hissed. "Someone is walking with us."

"Sí," said her host, "That's Detective Gomez. But we've no time for introductions now. Just stay close to me."

Nancy could now make out a ring of men closing in on the building. They became faintly visible in the pale street lights swathed in heavy fog. The group approached the large double doors on the end of the building and then paused while four policeman came up with a metal battering ram. With a quiet count of one, two, three, they slammed the ram into the door. The tremendous noise breaking through the night air made Nancy jump.

It was over within four swings. The door splintered and gave way. The police piled through while others guarded the windows and doors against anyone trying to escape.

Nancy ran inside right behind the battering ram, calling her father's name. But the police searchlights sweeping the single giant room revealed nothing. Except for dust, some old office furniture, and large storage cartons, the warehouse was empty. There was no sign of Carson Drew!

7

Where Is Carson Drew?

Nancy's face was stricken, her lower lip trembled, and she was on the verge of tears. As the lights were switched on in the warehouse, she heard a detective shout, "Don't touch anything! Don't touch anything!"

Señor Segovia was white with anger, the muscles in his jaw twitching. Nancy saw his lips moving and knew that he was saying something in Spanish but she didn't know what. When he had gotten some control over himself, he came over to where she was standing.

"I don't know what could have gone wrong," he said. "I'm sure your father was here!" He beat one clenched fist into the palm of his other hand.

"I know it, too," Nancy said. She was staring

49

at a stack of cartons with different names printed on them. On one, the letter D had been scribbled with a ball-point pen.

"You see—" Nancy traced the outline with her finger, "—how the lines are extended a bit? That's our signal. Dad made this mark to let us know he was here."

Señor Segovia studied the letter. "You are right!" he cried out excitedly. "That proves he *was* here. So my informant wasn't wrong. We just weren't quick enough!"

Nancy nodded. "I'd like to check around some more. Perhaps there's another clue we haven't found yet."

"Sure. Let's go ahead."

But an extensive search by both Nancy and the detectives brought nothing to light. When everyone was ready to leave, Señor Segovia turned to Nancy. "I'll have to stay in Miami and contact various people who might know something about this. Do you want to drive the Volkswagen home or shall I have the police take you?"

"I'll drive, thank you," Nancy said. "I remember the way quite well."

"Good. I'll call you as soon as I have more information."

The search party left the warehouse, and

minutes later Nancy was on her way back to the mansion. Her mind was racing and something was nagging her about the clue she had found, but she couldn't put her finger on it. Finally, she realized what it was. She remembered storage cartons in the warehouse all standing neatly in a row. Different names were printed on them. The one with the letter D bore the inscription "Belfont." Had her father chosen that particular carton for a reason? Was Belfont the place he had been taken?

"Belfont," Nancy said aloud. "It sounds like a hotel. Maybe it's out of business and the company that owns the warehouse bought things from them. I'd better find out!"

She pulled up in front of a restaurant and went inside to use the telephone. Quickly, she dialed the Miami police department. A sleepy voice answered and she asked for Señor Segovia.

"He isn't here," was the curt answer.

"May I speak to Detective Gomez, please?" Nancy said.

"He's not here, either. Who is this?"

"Nancy Drew."

"Well, you'd better call back in the morning."

"Tell me, where's the Hotel Belfont?" Nancy pressed.

"Belfont? There's no such thing. There was a hotel in town by that name, but it's been closed for several years now," the policeman replied.

"Can you tell me where it is?"

"I don't remember the street. All I know is that it's in a rundown area."

"Perhaps someone else knows the address?" Nancy continued, not wanting to give up.

There was a moment of silence, then the officer came back on the line. "It's on Huston Street. But as I said before, it's in a bad part of town. You wouldn't want to go there, especially at night."

"Thanks," Nancy said, and hung up. She went into the dining room and asked several people how to get to Huston Street. Finally, one of the patrons was able to give her directions. Before he, too, could warn her about the neighborhood, she thanked him and ran back to her car.

On the way to the hotel, she became worried. Maybe I should have told that policeman what it's all about and asked for an escort, she thought. Oh, well, it's too late now. I don't want to waste any more time. Dad might be in bad trouble!

Finally, she found herself in the middle of broken and sagging buildings. Trash cans were knocked over on the sidewalk and two cats started a fight down an alley to her right. She stopped the car and let her eyes sweep all around her while her ears picked up each new and strange noise of the night. From somewhere, she could hear a radio and she saw shadowy lights here and there. But there were no other human beings in sight and no building that had been painted or cared for during the past several years.

On the opposite side of the street a bit further down, her headlights picked out the letters BE FON HOTEL. She shivered. What a terrible place for her father to be held captive! She got out her flashlight and walked away from the car.

Crash!

Nancy almost jumped out of her skin. Wide-eyed and breathing hard, her back against a wall, she looked quickly left and right to see what had made the dreadful noise. Then she recognized the source of the racket. A garbage can rolled out of an alleyway, teetered on the edge of the curb, crashed into the gutter and came to rest.

A cat or dog probably knocked it over, Nancy thought. But she couldn't be sure and she felt the palms of her hands grow moist. What a difference between this scene and the huge bathtub at the Segovia mansion, with the black soap and the lovely, soft towels!

She was beginning to feel despair and panic now. Suppose the Belfont clue was not correct after all? Suppose Señor Segovia had already found out where Carson Drew was *really* being held? Suppose someone came out of the dark and attacked her?

But Nancy resolutely pushed those thoughts out of her mind. Squaring her shoulders, she walked up to the decrepit building that had once apparently been a respectable hotel. When she got there, a new shock awaited her. Every door and window was boarded over with wood and metal. There was no way to get in!

Once again, Nancy felt like giving up on her lonely effort. She considered calling the police, but finding a phone booth in this neighborhood was like trying to find gold. There simply were no phones visible.

She continued to examine the Belfont, bit by bit. Finally, she walked up on the big, decaying porch, feeling the boards sag under her feet. She carefully checked the doors and windows to see if there were some crack, some opening where she could pry away the boards and the metal in order to squeeze inside. But there was nothing.

Then she went back and looked up at the

second story. There was a roof over the first-floor porch, and the windows on the second floor were not boarded. But she saw that it would be impossible to climb up the shiny, smooth pillars that supported the roof.

"If Dad's really in there, the crooks must have taken him through some kind of entrance," she said softly. "Of course, they'd make sure it's well hidden. If only I could find it!"

She stepped back on the porch again and suddenly felt her heel sink into the flooring. Startled, she leaped to the side. Then she carefully shielded her flashlight and turned it on the spot where the wood had given way.

Of course! Trying to go through the doors and windows was foolish because the wood was relatively new and the galvanized metal was firmly in place. But the original wood of the hotel, particularly the floor of the porch, was badly rotted. Perhaps she could get in by simply pulling away a few boards!

Eagerly, Nancy dropped to her knees and felt around. She found the spot with the hole, reached in with her fingers, and got a grip on the edge of the broken board. Then she pulled. Groaning, the board came up, broke, and sent her sprawling backwards!

8

Rats

To Nancy, the noise was like a Fourth of July firecracker. For a full ten seconds, she lay back against the wall, convinced that she had awakened the entire neighborhood. If the crooks were actually holding her father in the Belfont, they must surely be looking for her by now!

But then Nancy took a deep breath. "Get hold of yourself," she whispered. Probably, the noise had not been nearly so loud as she thought. Apparently, it had done nothing to arouse the neighbors, since not even a dog barked in response.

Carefully, she got back up on her knees and felt for the hole she had made. She found that it was a good six inches wide and almost two feet long. Thank heavens for the big, wide boards they used in those old buildings! If she could pry loose one more, she could probably squeeze through the opening.

She felt around for the next board. Luckily, it was almost completely rotted away. It came loose in her hands with half of it crumbling. She noticed a whiff of musty air rising out of the hole. Now, if she could just squeeze through!

"Oh!" Nancy groaned. "If only I had dieted a little more the night before we left River Heights, instead of eating all that pizza and pistachio ice cream!"

She started to put her feet through the hole, and then stopped. What was she doing, dropping through a hole on the porch of this terrible, old hotel? How did she know what was waiting for her below? It could be anything!

Hastily pulling her feet back, she reached for her flashlight and flicked it on. There was a dirt floor not far below her. Of course, she thought, there's just a crawlspace under the porch. The real basement probably starts back ten feet at the hotel wall.

Nancy again put her feet through the hole and disappeared under the porch. Then she moved slowly toward the building, looking for an opening. What if they had nailed up everything down here, too? But she dismissed that idea when a worse thought struck her. Suppose the place *had* no basement? Houses were often constructed that way in Florida because the closeness of the sea made it hard to keep the water out.

But to her relief, she found an unboarded window with all the glass broken out. She shone her flashlight through and detected the basement floor about four feet down. Quickly, she crawled through the opening, and felt a heavy pipe just to her right. Putting her hands around it, she pulled her hips and legs through the window, hung for a moment, then dropped to the floor.

She found herself in the dirtiest cellar she had ever seen. It was heaped with boxes and barrels and cans. Every known type of junk and refuse was piled and thrown about in heaps and hillocks. The dust lay almost a half inch thick, sending up clouds when she moved.

"Boy," Nancy said, half aloud. "If Hannah could see this. What a cleaning she'd give it." But thinking of the Drews' beloved housekeeper made her remember her father. He probably was somewhere in this awful place, and she had to find him!

Carefully, Nancy got to her feet and began moving through the debris. She had taken two or three tentative steps when she heard an uproar of snarls and squeals. A dozen soft but heavy-feeling bodies exploded around her, banging into her legs. Nancy knew from the horrible sound emerging from under her right foot that she had stepped on the tail of a rat! Apparently, she had walked directly through a nest of rats that now seemed on all sides of her!

Somehow, she had the presence of mind not to scream. Instead, she simply took off as if she were running the hundred-yard dash, diving through the tangled jungle of the basement until she had put some distance between her and the rats.

She had learned about rodents as a result of a school study she had done on their habits. Therefore, she was aware of the fact that people's fear of rats often got out of control. Rats avoided humans whenever they could and never attacked anyone if they could run away instead. But a rat whose tail had been stepped on had every reason to believe that *it* was being attacked. Nancy considered it a real miracle she had not been bitten before getting away from the nest.

She now shone her flashlight everywhere as she walked, not only on the floor but along the shelves, where a rat might be strolling or sitting. But the animals had been warned, and she felt more and more assured that they had all gone into hiding.

Again her thoughts went to her father. Suppose he were tied up, helpless, somewhere? Suppose he had been left on the floor with those rats around? They wouldn't bother anyone who could move, but what would happen to a person bound hand and foot?

Nancy shuddered and climbed up the stairs to the first floor. She hurried from room to room, shielding her light, listening cautiously, waiting for some sound or sight that would give her a clue as to Carson Drew's whereabouts.

Then, up ahead, she saw a faint light. It was only a tiny sliver of yellow under a door. Her heart pounded. It had to be her father and his captors! Who else would be in this place at this time of night?

Creeping slowly up to the door, Nancy put her ear to it and listened. She heard rough, guttural voices. She strained to hear her father's among them, but in vain. Out of desperation she grew bold and pushed the door slightly to create a crack to see through.

Peering in, she gasped. Her father was sitting upright in a chair to which he was bound. There was a cut on his head, and some blood had dried on his forehead, but otherwise he seemed unhurt.

Nancy's heart beat loudly and her hands began to shake.

Two men were in the room with Mr. Drew. One, an extremely tall, thin man looked like a cadaver since his skin was so white that it was almost transparent. The other, also tall, was swarthy, with a mustache and beard.

Desperately, Nancy searched her mind for some way to distract the crooks so she could free her father and escape. But before she could put any of her schemes into action, she felt a powerful arm grab her right wrist. Her hand was forced up behind her back and she was propelled into the room, a captive!

9

Nancy's Ruse

"This makes it perfect," came the grating voice of the swarthy man. "Now we've got both the lawyer-father and the detective-daughter!"

The cadaverous-looking crook laughed in a peculiar, almost hiccuping manner. "Just the way Mac said it would work out."

"Shut up about Mac," said the swarthy man. "Can't you keep your mouth closed? Here, tie up the girl. Just like her father. Peas in a pod."

The thin man laughed again. "Yeah, peas in a pod. That's right."

"Shut up," said the swarthy man.

Nancy had no choice but to submit to the ropes being tied around her. She tensed her wrists and ankles against the bonds, making her muscles as tight as possible. It was an old escape artist's trick she had learned. Later, when the knots had been made, she could relax her muscles and feel a slight loosening of the ropes that, if she were lucky, would enable her to slip out of them. It didn't work all the time, but it was worth a try.

Nancy looked over at her father, who had a gag in his mouth. "Can't you at least take the gag out?" she pleaded with the men. "No one can hear us down here. It's so unnecessary."

"Don't tell us how to run our business!" the swarthy man grumbled. "Behave yourself, or we'll gag you, too."

Nancy's mind raced desperately. Perhaps she could put up a bold front and fool them. Tossing her hair defiantly, she said, "You know, no matter what you do to us, you won't be able to save your gang. You're finished."

The man who had twisted her arm was still standing in back of her in the semidarkness. Now he spoke for the first time. "I never did hear a woman run off at the mouth the way this girl does. Let's gag her."

"Shut up," said the swarthy man.

Nancy took a deep breath. "You have me and my father as captives. We're helpless. You can do anything you want to us. But you *won't*."

"Don't be too sure," the swarthy man rasped.

"Isn't it bad enough that you can already be charged with kidnapping? Are you fully aware of what the penalty is for kidnapping in the state of Florida? You'll get life imprisonment, at least. Now, if you let us go, we won't prosecute. Just set us free and that will be the end of it."

"No one's going to charge us with kidnapping." The swarthy man grinned. "No one's going to know!"

"Ah, but the police do know, and they're on their way here right now. You honestly don't think that I'd come here alone without telling them, do you?"

"But that's exactly what you would do, Nancy Drew! That's your method. We've studied you and your father, you see. We've studied you very closely."

"Yeah," said the tall, cadaverous man. "The Brotherhood of the Vulture has checked you out!"

Nancy started at the words. The swarthy man lost his patience with his colleague, letting fly a stream of insults and cuffing him about the head and shoulders.

"Stupid fool!" he screamed. "You keep quiet!

Stop dribbling words before you get us all in trouble, do you hear me?"

His cohort nodded, shuffled, and said nothing. At last, the swarthy man turned back to Nancy. "Well, now you've heard of the Brotherhood of the Vulture. But knowing a name won't do you any good."

"Oh, yes, it does," Nancy said coolly. "It tells me just who was behind the effort to stop me from coming to Fort Lauderdale. You must really be afraid if you're willing to go to these extremes."

Her captor dismissed her statement with a careless wave of his hand. "You're finished, Nancy Drew. When they find you and your father, it'll look like you had an accident. No one will ever know what happened."

"Someone will know very soon. What time is it, please?"

The thin man looked at his watch. "Eleven twenty-seven," he replied.

"Good," Nancy declared. "You have exactly three minutes of freedom left, because at eleven-thirty you're going to hear axes biting into the doors here and half the police in the state of Florida are going to come pouring through!"

Her heart was beating so fast she could hardly get her breath, but she knew that everything hinged on her ability to make them believe what she was saying. Mentally, she was kicking herself for not having let the police know.

The swarthy man simply laughed at her. But his thin friend began to pluck at his clothes nervously. Nancy knew that he was the one she had to concentrate on. She turned and looked at him.

"You don't really want to go to jail, do you?" she asked. "I can see you just came out recently. Your white skin betrays you. How do you feel about going back?"

The thin man coughed. "Pedro, we oughta go. I don't want no jail rap, not again. We can watch the place from outside, and if she was bluffing, we can always come back. They're—"

"Shut up! Stop calling me by my name, you moron!"

"I'm sorry. But listen—"

Just then, there was a crashing noise in the basement. It startled Nancy and her father as much as their captors.

"I'm getting out of here!" the thin man cried and rushed to the door. Pedro hesitated only a second, then followed, and so did their other colleague. As their footsteps died away, Nancy quickly tried to loosen her bonds. The thin man, as she expected, had been the softest of the three in all ways. In tying her up, he had not pulled the ropes very tight. After a bit of exertion, Nancy freed her right hand. It was then only a matter of moments before she had extricated herself completely and was able to remove the gag from her father's mouth. He let out a great gasp.

"Oh, Nancy, thank you. I'm so glad you came. Are the police really following you?"

"No, they don't even know I'm here. That crash downstairs must have been the rats kicking something over. Boy, am I glad it happened just at the right time!"

She furiously worked on the bonds that tied her father. "We'd better get out of here quickly, though. The men might come back once they realize I was only bluffing."

"I hope they were scared enough to have run a long way," Mr. Drew said.

"Are you strong enough to walk?" Nancy asked. "You look so pale."

"I'd *better* be able to walk," her father said with a weak grin. "Come on."

The two hurried out of the room and back into the basement. Nancy helped Mr. Drew down the stairs, but by the time they reached the window, his circulation had improved and he was able to pull himself up. A few moments later, the two surfaced on the dilapidated porch. Everything seemed quiet around them.

"See that old Volkswagen across the street?" Nancy whispered. "It belongs to Señor Segovia. He gave it to me to drive back to the mansion. Let's make a run for it."

Her father nodded. "But our three friends may lie in wait for us. Let me just grab something in case we're attacked."

He had seen a piece of lead pipe and realized it would be perfect for his purpose. Quickly, he picked it up. "Now I feel a little safer," he said. "Let's go!"

The two emerged from the hole in the porch and ran toward the car as fast as they could. Nancy slipped behind the wheel and an instant later took off in a cloud of dust.

Her father rubbed his aching ankles. "Nancy, this was a wonderful rescue. How did you know where to find me?"

She told him about their search in the warehouse and the clue she had found. Her father smiled. "I was going to draw an arrow from the letter D to the word Belfont, but at that moment, the crooks turned to me and I almost didn't manage to hide my pen in time. I'm glad you managed to find me anyway."

"So am I."

"But Nancy, I want you to promise me something."

"Yes, Dad?"

"Never, never do something like this on your own again. It's much too dangerous. Always inform the police and have them help you."

Nancy nodded. "I know I should have done that. But I was so excited when I figured out the Belfont clue, and the man at headquarters who answered the phone wasn't very cooperative—"

"With perseverance, you could have found someone who'd have helped you," her father pointed out.

"I know," Nancy said ruefully. "I won't do it again."

"Pull up by that diner over there," Mr. Drew said after a while. "I want to notify the police and Señor Segovia of my rescue."

Nancy did, and he went inside to a public telephone. When he came out, he smiled. "I was lucky to reach Señor Segovia," he said.

"What did he say?" Nancy asked eagerly.

"Well, he was delighted to hear that I had escaped. When I told him *you* had helped me, he was absolutely flabbergasted. He's on his way home now, and he'll tell us there what he's found out in the meantime."

When they arrived at the Segovia mansion, they went to their rooms for a few moments to clean up, then met Señor Segovia and the girls in the living room. Bess and George hugged Nancy and her father excitedly and congratulated their friend on her spectacular rescue. Then Nancy told the details of her adventure.

Señor Segovia was surprised at her clever deduction that her father had been held in the Belfont, but also warned her not to undertake a search like this alone in the future.

"I did some investigating, too," he· said. "I found out you were relocated, Carson, because the gang was worried that the warehouse wasn't safe enough, even though the company who owns it doesn't use it much anymore. But my informant didn't know where you had been moved to. It took Nancy to find that out!"

"It was just a hunch," Nancy said with an embarrassed smile.

"Well, I'm willing to take great stock in your hunches," Señor Segovia said. "You may be of much help in our investigation. And now, even though it's late, I just want to explain very briefly to you and your friends what it is that we're up against!"

10

Mrs. Palmer Lashes Out!

After making his guests comfortable and having seen to it that they were served cooling drinks, Señor Segovia outlined the details of his struggle against the stamp smugglers.

"As a representative of the government," he began, "I was assigned to direct the investigation of the smuggling ring. But the crooks are so bold and contemptuous that they actually filed a multi-million-dollar lawsuit against me, charging me with libel and slander for statements I allegedly made in public."

"The reason for this," Nancy spoke up, "is probably to keep you busy with legal matters so you can't probe the gang's dealings."

"That's correct," Señor Segovia went on. "They charged me with interfering in what they claim is a perfectly legitimate operation. That's when I called in your father."

"As I began to gather evidence against the gang," Mr. Drew took up the story, "they became worried and kidnapped me."

"That was a bad mistake on their part," Señor Segovia said. "It made it very obvious that their claim of legitimacy is ridiculous. I'm convinced it only happened because Stroessner is in South America. But he's coming back tonight, and when he does, there'll be some fireworks in his outfit."

"Who's Stroessner?" Nancy questioned.

"Otto Stroessner is the big man who runs the entire rotten syndicate," Mr. Drew put in. "He's a big bull of a man with a bald head and a monocle. But he has impeccable manners and is charming and gracious. The ladies who don't know him better think he's a romantic figure. Those who do know him realize that he is one of the top criminals in the world. He's a man who will stop at nothing."

"Yes," Señor Segovia agreed. "He's also a man who carefully calculates his every move. And he would never have approved your kidnapping, Carson. Someone else did that."

"McConnell," the lawyer said. "They mentioned it."

"Who's McConnell?" Bess asked.

Señor Segovia laughed. "This session is supposed to brief you on what's happening and we keep dropping names you don't know. Brian McConnell is Stroessner's second in command here in the States. Why, I don't know. He's not Stroessner's type of man at all. He's a hotheaded soldier of fortune who sells himself to the highest bidder. He's been a smuggler, a gun runner, a guerrilla leader. But he has no sense. He's all bravado and does foolhardy things, thinking it will please Stroessner, and it never does."

"Why does Stroessner put up with him?" Nancy asked.

"Because McConnell saved his life once. Stroessner was almost executed in one of the smaller Latin American countries after helping to organize a revolution. McConnell got him out of jail and flew him to the United States. So Stroessner is stuck with Mac."

"And McConnell pulled this kidnapping?" George asked.

"Yes. But I don't think we'll see him around too much longer. There's a limit to Stroessner's gratitude." Señor Segovia went on to describe how Stroessner had built up a criminal empire and had directed the theft of many major stamp collections in the world. He had thrown the stamp market into absolute chaos, for not only had he begun to dispose of the stamps at extremely high prices, but word had leaked out that he was planning to counterfeit the most valuable of his stolen property.

"If the counterfeiting proves as good as the other schemes he has had, there is simply no doubt that the market will be destroyed," Señor Segovia declared. "No one will know whether he's buying a real stamp or a phony one."

"The losses now are running toward the billion-dollar mark," Mr. Drew said. "The latest stamp that was stolen was a heretofore unknown copy of the Penny Black, issued in the nineteenth century by what was then the British colony of Guiana."

"You mean, no one realized this stamp existed?" Nancy asked.

"That's right. The only known copy was in the hands of a wealthy collector. Then another one was found in an ordinary stamp album in Buenos Aires, stashed away in someone's attic for a long time. After its discovery, only a few days passed until the stamp was stolen by two armed men making their getaway in a helicopter. This, of course, was a great shock to all philatelists—as stamp collectors are called. We feel that Stroessner's gang was involved."

"Why has Stroessner made his headquarters in southern Florida?" Nancy asked.

Señor Segovia spread his hands. "Since the very earliest days of the first Spanish explorers, Florida has been recognized as a paradise for smugglers. The long coastline, indented by bays and rivers and streams and with lots of islands and hundreds of square miles of swamps and wilderness, it's one of the toughest areas for customs and border patrol people to cover."

"Smugglers come in by sea, by land, under the sea, and by air," Carson Drew added. "It's very difficult to catch them."

"What is Stroessner's so-called legitimate business?" Nancy inquired.

"He's a stamp dealer," Señor Segovia replied. "He has a very thorough knowledge of the trade, and contacts all over the world. He knows who owns what, and where the most valuable collections are. That's why we have to get him. We have to find him standing there with the evidence in his hands, so to speak. With a man as tricky and careful as Stroessner, that's very hard."

"There are two ways to do it," Mr. Drew spoke up. "Either we catch him with the evidence, which is possible but extremely difficult to accomplish, or we capture one or two of his top men and use their testimony against him. We have to try both ways."

"What about the counterfeiting?" Nancy asked. "Why and how is he going to do that?"

"Well," Señor Segovia replied, "as to why he's doing it, the answer is, very quick money. He could duplicate, let's say, the fifty most valuable stamps in the world and make twenty of each. Then he could put them on sale in hundreds of cities all over the globe on the same day."

"Before the stamp collectors have time to check with one another and compare," Nancy added.

"Exactly. By the time anyone knows that there's something wrong, he runs off with millions of dollars and thousands of collectors are cheated."

"Do you know whether he has started the counterfeiting already?" Nancy asked. Carson Drew smiled as he saw a familiar sparkle in her blue eyes. He knew it meant that she was hooked on a mystery.

"No," Señor Segovia replied. "We don't think he has started. We know the equipment has been moved into Florida. But he doesn't have a top man yet to do the work. We have police all over the world keeping tight checks on all leading counterfeiters who aren't in jail. The minute one of them disappears, it may mean he has started working for Stroessner. We must break up this ring before that happens."

"Where is the gang's headquarters?" Nancy asked.

"We don't know. We do know Stroessner is living in a fine house in Fort Lauderdale, telling the government that he's just a legitimate stamp dealer."

"That's right," Mr. Drew added. "From time to time, he even has the nerve to wave to Señor Segovia across a crowded restaurant table or to send a bottle of wine to the Segovia table with an insulting note attached."

Further questions from the girls brought them no additional information, so they finally decided to go to bed. As Nancy started up the stairs for her bedroom, she was interrupted by the maid carrying a telephone.

"For me?" Nancy asked, surprised.

The maid nodded, and the girl took the receiver hesitantly, glancing at Señior Segovia, who put his finger to his lips as he waved to Mr. Drew and they went to pick up an extension.

"Hello, my foot!" came a strong but obviously aged female voice on the other end of the line. "What's going on, Nancy Drew? You've been in this city for quite a while and you haven't called me."

"Mrs. Palmer?" Nancy cried. "Oh, I'm so sorry. I—"

"Sorry, my bumbershoot. When I hire a detective, I expect her to be on the job right away. This is an outrage! I don't believe Carson ever took a switch to you!"

"But my father was kidnapped," Nancy blurted, knowing no other way to stop the tide of words coming over the phone.

"Kidnapped! It's bad enough you're late. If you can't keep your own father from being kidnapped, what kind of a detective are you? You're not too old to spank, you know. I'll expect you here at seven o'clock tomorrow morning. Sharp."

"Seven o'clock!"

"Good night, Miss Drew. And bring your magnifying glass or whatever you detectives use."

Nancy heard a click and she sank against the wall.

"Phew," she exclaimed and looked at Señor Segovia and her father, who came up to her after having listened to every word. "I think that I've just met my toughest client yet!"

Mr. Drew chuckled. "She's really a very nice lady," he said. "You'll like her once you get to know her."

"I hope so," the girl murmured as she went off to bed.

Nancy slept soundly, without dreams or nightmares. Finally, she awoke to the sounds of laughter in the pool area beneath her windows.

She lay for a moment, stretching luxuriously under the lovely pink sheets. Voices drifted to her but she was still too sleepy to recognize them. Then, pulling her knees up she made the effort and got out of bed. She looked out the window and noticed the boys frolicking with Bess and George.

The boys! What were they doing here already? Nancy wondered. Then a terrible thought struck her. She looked at her watch.

"Ten o'clock!" she cried out loud. "And I was supposed to be at Mrs. Palmer's at seven! The maid forgot to wake me up!"

11

Puzzling Burglaries

Quickly, Nancy got dressed and hurried out to the patio where Carson Drew and Señor Segovia lounged over their breakfast.

"Dad!" she cried. "I'm late for Mrs. Palmer!"

Carson Drew laughed, took his daughter's hand, and pulled her into a chair beside him. "Relax, Nancy. I called her this morning and told her what happened last night. I said you were exhausted and would be over later."

"Wow!" Nancy fell back in her chair. "Thanks, Dad. I wouldn't want to upset her a second time. Once was enough. But what are the boys doing here? When did they get in?"

"They had an exciting adventure, those young men," Señor Segovia replied. "Perhaps they'd better tell you themselves. Here they come."

Her friends, having seen her at last, ran whooping and yelling from the pool, all of them dripping with water.

"Ned," Nancy asked, "what happened?"

"Oh, we had a problem. After we left you, we got as far as central New Jersey. Then Dave said he wanted to stop at this terrific little farm right off the highway, where they sold great fruit."

"Yes," Burt added, "and soon we were in mud up to our axles. It took us four hours to get a tow truck to pull us out. In fact, the first truck they sent also got stuck, and the second one had to rescue both of us."

"Then," Dave put in, "by the time we got to Washington, the poor old Land Rover decided to call it quits. It stopped running, because the transmission was ruined. The only thing we could do was leave the car in a repair shop and climb on a plane. We got the first flight out this morning and arrived here before anyone was up."

"Sounds perfectly reasonable." Nancy giggled. "I bet you're sorry now that you were bragging so about beating us!"

"Sorry. Humble. Apologetic," Ned said, and the three boys bowed their heads as the girls laughed.

"Hey, come on into the pool, Nancy, it's terrific," Ned invited.

"I will," she said, "later."

Her friends ran back to the water as Nancy ate her breakfast and thought about the smugglers. She suddenly recalled something she and her father had not talked about before.

"The Brotherhood of the Vulture," she mused. "Remember, Dad, those crooks talking about the Brotherhood of the Vulture last night?"

Señor Segovia frowned and stirred his coffee. Then he looked at Carson Drew. The attorney sighed and nodded. "Yes, my captors mentioned it, so I suppose we should discuss it. Ricardo, would you like to explain?"

Señor Segovia rubbed his chin. "Well, Nancy," he said, "the Brotherhood of the Vulture is a criminal organization that has sprung up in Latin America. Actually, it's a revival of a group that existed more than a century ago and then disappeared. Apparently, some modern crooks have decided to start it again."

"And is Stroessner involved with it?" Nancy asked.

"Yes," Señor Segovia replied. "We don't know whether he's the head or just one of the more powerful bosses, but we do know he's part of it."

He fell silent. Nancy looked from him to her father. "Don't you want to tell me more?" she asked.

"We don't know any more," Mr. Drew replied.

"Do they have a symbol that looks like a great bird with its wings partly folded?"

"Yes," her father answered. "How did you know?"

"Because," Nancy said, "I had a terrible dream the night before we left that a great, black bird was chasing me through Fort Lauderdale. Then, the man who sabotaged our airplane must have stuck one of them on our plane."

"You didn't tell me someone sabotaged your plane!" her father exclaimed. "When you called, all you mentioned was that there was some trouble. I thought you were talking about a mechanical failure!"

"Well, it turned out that it wasn't. Someone drained half the gas out of our tank before we left. We had to land in the water off the coast of South Carolina with a dead stick. Fred Blaine came out and rescued us. I didn't have a chance to tell you because you got yourself kidnapped, Dad."

Carson Drew heaved a sigh of relief. "At least your luck held and I'm grateful for that."

Señor Segovia added "I haven't had time to tell you either, Carson, that the vulture symbol appeared on the inside roof of the limousine I sent for Nancy. My driver tore it off but not before it frightened the girls, I'm sorry to say."

"What does it mean," Nancy asked, "when they put the symbol on things like that?"

"I think it's a scare tactic," her father replied. "Possibly, they're trying to get to me through you."

Nancy nodded. "Perhaps they figure if we get worried about the black buzzard, we won't have our minds on catching the gang at their dirty work."

Bess and George ran up at that moment. "Hey, are you going to eat all morning?" George asked. "We need help if we're having another water fight with these three monsters." She pointed to the boys.

"Oh, I'm sorry," Nancy said. "But I have to go see Mrs. Palmer. You want to come?"

"Sure," George said. "If we stay here, those guys are going to drown us anyway."

When the girls broke the news to the boys, they offered to go along. But Señor Segovia suggested that they might like to spend the rest of the morning taking his yacht out through the canal onto the ocean. Ned, Dave, and Burt quickly agreed after their friends assured them they weren't needed at Mrs. Palmer's, and with a few shouted good-byes, hurried down to the dock.

"Well!" Bess said with an exaggerated flounce of the wraparound skirt she had just put on. "If I'd known they'd be so heartbroken about us leaving, I wouldn't have agreed to go."

Nancy and George burst into laughter. "That shows how much we count, doesn't it?" George said as they followed the chauffeur André, who this time led them to a light blue limousine instead of the gray one. He was more relaxed now that Mr. Drew had been found, but he drove too slowly and carefully for the girls, who were bursting to see Mrs. Palmer's house and the strange and somewhat intimidating old woman who lived there.

When André finally pulled up and got out to open the door, the girls leaned forward to stare at the place. There it stood, ominous, gloomy, and three stories high with two turrets. It was surely full of big, impressive rooms, winding staircases, and strange creaking sounds.

"Brrr—" Bess said, hugging herself with her arms as if she had a chill. "I wouldn't want to spend the night alone in there."

"Me neither," George agreed. "But not because I'd be afraid. It's just that I've gotten used to greater luxury at Señor Segovia's!"

The girls laughed, then Nancy led her friends along the concrete walk up the five big steps to the front porch. She grabbed the large door knocker and let it go. The resulting *boom* reverberated so loudly that it made Bess jump. But she smiled as soon as Susan McAfee appeared to welcome the trio. "I'm so relieved you got here," she said.

"I wish I felt relieved." Nancy chuckled. "Is Mrs. Palmer ready?"

"Yes. And don't worry, she won't bite."

The girls followed Miss McAfee's clickety-clacking high heels through a parlor decorated entirely in mauve into a huge, old-fashioned kitchen.

"Would you like some tea or soda?" Susan asked. "Mrs. Palmer will be right with you."

The girls declined, and chatted with Susan for a few moments.

"Perhaps you think it unusual that Mrs. Palmer is greeting you in her kitchen instead of one of the more formal rooms," Susan McAfee said.

"Yes," Bess replied. "I was wondering about that."

"Well, this means you're 'in.' You're practically family when she invites you into her kitchen. Why, she . . ."

"That's enough of that, Susan!"

All four girls jumped at the sound of the voice from the doorway. Wheeling around, they saw Mrs. Palmer, erect and regal with her gray hair piled high on her head in great swirls.

Though Bess's heart went into her mouth, she was so impressed by the old lady that she almost curtsied as one would before a queen.

"Oh, Mrs. Palmer," Susan cried, her cheeks reddening.

"For goodness sake, don't look as if you're going to be executed. I don't mind your telling the girls that the kitchen is my sanctum and only the best people ever enter it. There now, you must feel honored and delighted and all that sort of rubbish. Aha . . ."

She peered from Bess to George, then her eyes fastened on Nancy. "I need glasses to read but I don't need them to spot a Drew. Those blue eyes are an absolute giveaway. They're almost exactly the color of my own. That, plus the titian hair tells me that you're Nancy. Your great-grandmother had hair like that, too, you know. Yes, exactly like that!" Mrs. Palmer rapped her cane on the floor for emphasis.

The girls stood fixedly, not knowing whether they had permission to speak. Then Nancy smiled. "I'm glad to meet you, Mrs. Palmer. I've heard so much about you."

"Ah, none of your charm, girl. I know what you heard about me. Cantankerous old lady with one foot in the grave and another on a banana peel."

"Oh, no," Nancy protested.

"Well, never mind. I *am* cantankerous sometimes. Now, introduce me to your friends."

"Of course," Nancy said. "This is George Fayne and Bess Marvin."

"Welcome. I assume I may speak freely in the presence of George and Bess? Well, good. Now everyone sit down."

The girls did as bidden but the regal old woman remained standing, ramrod stiff. "I don't sit," she said. "I never sit if I can stand. I never stand if I can walk. And up until a few years ago, I never walked when I could run. That's why I outlived all my friends, who used to sit around eating petits fours and drinking tea and wasting their lives on nonsense."

Mrs. Palmer paced back and forth as she talked, her long skirt almost touching the floor. She moved with small steps and so little motion that she almost looked as if she were on rollers. Bess nudged George, and they both suppressed grins.

"Now then," Mrs. Palmer said, "let's proceed with the business at hand. Some utter fools, for reasons we do not yet know, keep breaking into this house. They steal nothing. They don't really damage anything either, except one vase that they broke, probably by accident. They have done this time and again, and I'm becoming sick of it."

She paused a moment, then continued. "I have complained, most vociferously, to the police, the state police, the mayor, and the governor. They have posted a guard, but frankly, I find it annoying to have someone watching my home, even if he's on my side. So today, knowing that you're going to be on the job, I asked the authorities to remove the officer."

Nancy was somewhat taken aback. "I appreciate your trust," she said, "but I'm afraid that the police are much better at that sort of thing than I am. I simply try to find clues and determine who has been committing these burglaries. But I'm really not capable of guarding this house day and night by myself."

Mrs. Palmer waved her hand airily. "Nonsense! The very fact that you are on the job already has the crooks scared stiff. I have no doubt that you shall have the case solved within twenty-four hours."

Nancy sighed, and then, realizing it was useless to argue, she got out her note pad and began to question Mrs. Palmer, seeking every bit of information she could gather. Where had Mrs. Palmer been each time a burglary occurred? She had been out. When did the burglaries take place? Always in the evening. What about the servants?

Mrs. Palmer grew stiff at the last question. "I have a butler, a maid, and a gardener, and they're all beyond reproach. Besides, none of them were home during the burglaries, except Errol, the butler, was here the first time. He chased the crooks but didn't catch them. Hit his head in the process, poor man."

"I'll need to speak to him," Nancy said.

"He's not here now," Mrs. Palmer said stiffly.

Nancy did not press the matter for the present, deciding to get back to the subject later when she had better learned how to handle the old lady.

"All right," she said. "Let's see what we

have." She riffled through her notes. Mrs. Palmer arched her neck and looked at the pages.

"May I congratulate you," she said. "Most people today write as if they were handcuffed. But your handwriting is precise and beautiful."

"Well," Nancy said, "that's more a matter of necessity than of good training. When I first started, I used to scrawl my notes. Then I found I couldn't read some of them, and a detective who can't read her notes may as well take up another profession. So I forced myself to write neatly."

Mrs. Palmer waved her hand. "No modesty. Whatever the reason, I find it admirable. Now you were saying?"

"Well," Nancy continued, "it's obvious we have one of two possibilities here. The burglars are looking for something specific, which they believe is in this house. Now, either it *is* here or they have been misinformed, and it is not."

Mrs. Palmer nodded, showing signs of impatience. "Yes, yes."

"That's it," Nancy said. "Unless you actually *know* what it is they're looking for, but for some reason won't reveal it?"

12

An Inside Job?

Mrs. Palmer stared fiercely at Nancy for a long time, but the girl met her look and did not blanch. Then, slowly, the woman permitted herself a smile.

"Well, Nancy Drew, you really aren't afraid of me, are you? That's good. I can't bear people who are scared of me." She walked up and down, gesturing with her cane like a field marshal reviewing troops.

"No," she said, "I don't know what it is they are after. Money, silver, jewels, some pieces of paper they feel are valuable? I have no idea. I think they're just crazy."

"Or," Nancy said, "it could be that someone is trying to drive *you* crazy."

"Me!" Mrs. Palmer cried, laughing heartily.

"Drive me crazy? Oh, my. Half of Fort Lauderdale thinks I'm crazy already. Oh, no, I don't believe that."

Nancy tapped her pencil on the table and frowned.

"Maybe," Bess put in, "Mrs. Palmer's dismissal of the police guard was a good move after all."

The old woman turned to look at the girl, who sat back, a little abashed at having spoken up. But Mrs. Palmer motioned for her to continue.

"Well," Bess went on, "with no police, the crooks may try to get in the house again. We know they'll do it at night, because that's how they've always done it. It seems to me that all we have to do is to lay one of the famous Nancy Drew ambush scenes."

Mrs. Palmer walked over to Bess and raised her chin with one hand. "You are too pretty to be looking down so much. Don't be so shy. I admit it's refreshing to see a girl with downcast eyes. But save that for the boys. Among us girls, keep your head up, because you just had a very good idea."

Bess smiled, relieved and feeling good under the praise.

Nancy nodded. "That *was* a good idea, Bess. We'll start tonight."

"No," Mrs. Palmer objected. "I'm having company for dinner. But I shall let you know about tomorrow. Perhaps we can plan it then." She indicated that the interview was at an end. But Nancy did not get up.

"Mrs. Palmer," she said, "we haven't quite finished yet. There is still the matter of your servants and their reliability."

Mrs. Palmer snorted. "Really, Nancy. I won't discuss that because, as I said before, my servants are beyond reproach. Now that settles it."

Nancy shook her head. "You are too smart a woman to believe that. If you were in my place, you know very well that you would insist on knowing everything about everyone. It would be unforgivably sloppy detective work to ignore the servants."

Mrs. Palmer started to speak, stopped, and took a few paces. "Very well. But you are wasting your time."

"I hope so," Nancy said, "because I don't want to find that one of your people *is* involved. But I must learn the truth."

Mrs. Palmer nodded. "I think I'll sit down for this," she said, and took the chair that Nancy quickly brought to her.

"Now, what about the butler?" the young detective asked.

"Errol has been with me for thirty-three years. He is immaculate and impeccable in his duties. I have never known him to be rude."

"Has he ever been arrested?"

"Why on earth did you ask that?" Mrs. Palmer huffed.

"Because if he has been arrested or has a prison record it might . . ."

"It might cause the police to believe that he was a thief. Oh, really, Miss Drew!" The woman's tone was now icy.

"No, no, Mrs. Palmer, listen. If he had been arrested or has been in jail it doesn't mean that he's guilty. But perhaps someone knows about it and is now trying to blackmail him or implicate him in some way. Maybe he has even been threatened."

"My heavens," Mrs. Palmer marveled, her icy tone gone. "How your mind works! *Crack, crack, crack!* Amazing. But no, I tell you, Errol has never been in jail."

"Nor arrested?"

"No."

"Now, what happened when he encountered the burglars?"

"You can ask him, if you wish. I just heard the door and I'm sure that's Errol. Just a minute."

Mrs. Palmer went outside and returned with

a man in his fifties, who had a warm smile for the visitors.

After Mrs. Palmer had made the introductions, he said to Nancy, "It's so nice to meet you. I'm sure you'll be able to help us in this most annoying situation."

Nancy nodded, then asked, "I hear you were home during one of the burglaries."

"Only the first one," the butler replied. "In fact, I'm proud to say that I discovered the rascals but not in time to stop them. They stopped me, however." He pointed to his forehead where Nancy saw a scar.

"Oh, no!" she said. "Did they hit you?"

"I wish it were that heroic. No, I stormed down the stairs, shouting at them, hoping they'd run away since I was unarmed. But I tripped about halfway and did a couple of somersaults. Knocked me out, I'm afraid."

"Did you see what the intruders looked like?"

"No. There were two of them, but they wore stocking masks over their faces. All I know is that they were on the tall side. Anyway, I hope you're successful in putting an end to this nonsense."

"I'll try very hard, Errol," Nancy said.

The butler smiled and left the kitchen.

"What about the gardener?" Nancy asked Mrs. Palmer.

"Edward. He has been with me forty-seven years. Longer than the trees, he likes to say. Well, it's true. He planted everything you see around this house. Now don't tell me you suspect Edward. He's a perfect lamb and quiet as can be. He never misses church."

"And he has never been arrested or jailed?"

"Oh, no! He'd die of shame if they ever arrested him."

"And where was he at the time of the burglaries?"

"On vacation. Poor dear had a bad illness, so he went to recuperate at his sister's for a couple of weeks. But he's due to come home today."

"That leaves the maid," Nancy went on.

"Right," Mrs. Palmer said. "That's Odette. She's twenty-eight years old. Her mother worked for me for forty years. Oh, my. Impossible, Nancy. Forget about the servants."

"She's never been arrested?" Nancy pressed on.

"Yes, as a matter of fact, she has. It was a dreadful mistake, though. Many years ago, a salesman came to the door. Very persistent. He pushed past her and came right into my kitchen, trying to sell me aluminum ware. Well,

Odette is part French and has a very hot temper when angered. When the man refused to go, she attacked him with his own pots and pans. Beat him rather severely and almost destroyed his samples. He ran out of here with lumps all over him. But he came back with a policeman and said Odette had tried to murder him, which was a terrible exaggeration. We then charged the man with unlawful entry and trespassing, and everyone had to go to the police station."

"You, too?" Bess squeaked.

"Of course, me, too," said Mrs. Palmer. "I wouldn't have missed it for the world. Anyway, my lawyer had Odette free in no time."

"What happened to the salesman?" George asked, curious.

"Oh, we dropped the charges. Poor thing, he was so bruised and his pots were a mess. He'd been punished enough."

"May I talk to Odette?" Nancy asked.

"She has the day off."

Nancy nodded. "Can you tell me something about your servants' habits, Mrs. Palmer?"

"Habits?"

"Yes, or I should say, have there been any recent changes in their habits?"

"Oh, really, Nancy. I don't pry into my servants' lives."

"Of course not," the young detective said soothingly. "But did you notice any change in any of them in the last few months?"

Mrs. Palmer furrowed her brow and stared out the window. "I'm trying to think," she said. There was silence for a few moments, then she spoke again. "Odette has started an exercise class. And Errol has taken up boating. You know, motorboating. He does that a lot lately. Anything suspicious there?"

Nancy smiled but did not comment. "Mrs. Palmer, you've been very helpful. I think that's about all I need to ask right now. But as I come up with other questions, may I call you?"

"Why, of course," the woman replied. "If you like, I'll find out everyone's hat size and favorite color. My goodness. Detectives. Such a nosy group."

Susan McAfee winked at Nancy over Mrs. Palmer's shoulder, then came forward and escorted the girls out. As they passed through the parlor, Bess and George questioned Susan about the furnishings. Suddenly, Nancy heard a noise and was startled to see the mauve drapes move slightly. She glanced at the floor and noticed a pair of men's shoes beneath them! As she started toward them, the feet pulled out of sight!

13

Trapped!

Nancy stopped, letting the other girls get ahead of her. Her mind raced. Who could the intruder be, and where did he retreat to? Perhaps he was climbing out of the window!

She was just about to rush toward the spot where she had seen the shoes, when Errol stepped out from behind the heavy drapes. He held a dust cloth in one hand and a hammer in the other.

"I didn't mean to startle you," he said, "but these old windows jam badly. I had to give them a little rap with the hammer."

"Oh, that's all right, Errol," Nancy said, feeling a bit foolish.

Just then George called from the vestibule. "Come on, Nancy!"

"I'm coming," the young detective called back and joined her two friends in the hallway.

They said good-bye to Susan McAfee, then left the old Victorian house. André was standing next to the light blue limousine, waiting for them.

On the way back to the Segovia mansion, Nancy told the girls about seeing Errol behind the drapes. "He had a perfectly good explanation of what he was doing there. Yet, the way his feet were sticking out really gave me a scare."

"Maybe he was eavesdropping!" George said. "And he just used the story about the windows as an excuse!"

"I don't think so," Bess objected. "He's a perfectly sweet man."

"That's the impression I had," Nancy agreed. "But, you never know."

"And now," Bess said, "can we stop being detectives for a little while and become tourists? I'd like to swim and water ski and live it up in the sun!"

"I'd go for that," George agreed.

"That makes three of us," Nancy said. "Let's do it as soon as we get back."

"I hope the boys haven't splashed all the water out of the pool," Bess said.

"They couldn't," George reminded her. "Remember, they went off on that gorgeous yacht!"

In late afternoon, Nancy and the other girls were sitting by the pool when the yacht returned. As it hove to around a bend in the canal, the girls broke out in a laugh. Ned, Burt, and Dave were lying flat on their backs on deck chairs, dropping grapes into their mouths like so many Roman emperors.

"This is the only way to live!" Dave cried.

There was a lot of teasing and small talk, then the boys had a swim before they all heeded the warning cry, "Dinner in half an hour!" and hurried to their rooms to get dressed.

After dinner, Nancy said, "Anyone ready for Fort Lauderdale Beach?"

"Yes!" Bess exclaimed. "I thought you'd never mention it."

After calling good-bye to Señor Segovia and Carson Drew, the group started for Las Olas Boulevard that led directly to the beach. André was about to help them into the light blue limousine again, when Nancy stopped short.

"No," she said. "It's not far and we're getting spoiled. I'd rather walk."

"Oh, really?" Ned said. "I should think you'd have some pity for us *poor* people. I've never ridden in a light blue limousine before."

"But the walk will be good for us," George declared. "Honestly, you boys are so lazy."

"Lazy?" Burt cried. "Lazy? How would *you* like to push a Rover over half of New Jersey and then catch a plane in the wee hours of the morning?"

The kidding continued as they walked out the driveway. Behind them, Nancy noticed a tall, muscular man whom she had never seen before, and she stopped.

"Excuse me, but may I ask why you're following us?" she asked him.

The man smiled, crinkling the well-tanned, almost leathery skin of his face. "Not at all, Miss Drew. I'm Albert. I work for Señor Segovia and he's told me to go along with you folks and make sure that everything is all right."

"You mean, you're a bodyguard!"

"Yes ma'am, I guess you could call it that. I'm supposed to see you don't get hit by cars or eaten by alligators and things like that."

They all laughed, but Ned was uncomfortable with the situation. "We'll be all right," he declared. "We've got three men here who are capable of taking care of themselves."

Albert smiled. "I don't doubt that, Mr. Nickerson, and if it were up to me I wouldn't argue the point. But I work for Señor Segovia and when he tells me to do something I generally do it because I want to keep eating and wearing good boots." Albert smiled again. It was clear that no one was going to change his mind.

"Well, all right," Ned said, "but you won't make it obvious, will you?"

"No. You won't even know I'm around unless there's trouble. There are two other fellows who'll be with us. They're up ahead. You probably won't see them but we'll all be in the neighborhood in case any of Señor Stroessner's hoods decide to play rough."

With Albert drifting along behind them at a discreet distance, the boys besieged Nancy with questions.

"What's happening?" Burt asked. "We heard about your dad's kidnapping—"

"It's another case, isn't it?" Ned put in.

"Yes," Nancy replied. "Actually, it's two cases, mine and my father's. He and Señor Segovia are trying to track down stamp thieves while I'm supposed to find a bunch of burglars who don't steal anything."

"Tell us more," Burt urged.

"Later," Nancy said. "I promise. Now let's

relax and forget all about crooks, shall we?"

Reluctantly, her friends agreed as they walked along Las Olas Boulevard toward the sea. It was in the oldest part of the city and was filled with beautiful shops, all with canopies built out over the sidewalks so that shoppers could stroll for blocks without getting heatstroke from the strong Florida sun.

"I can smell the sea," Nancy said, tilting her head and inhaling deeply.

"All I hear is a roar," Bess said. "And it sounds more like a crowd than the ocean."

"It *is* a crowd," Dave told her. "There are thousands of students here on their spring break."

Weary policemen, on foot and on motorbikes, moved among the young people, trying to make paths for the few unsuspecting motorists who had taken the beach road, and were now crawling along at a snail's pace.

At last, Nancy and her friends reached the beach. They took off their shoes, waded in the water, and talked with several vacationers, mostly about the trials of getting to Fort Lauderdale in this busy season.

Finally, everyone agreed it was time for snacks and soft drinks. They made their way back to the street and managed to struggle into a restaurant and out again with a huge order of pizza, spare ribs, hamburgers, and Cokes. They took their food to a vacant corner that Ned found in an alley between two apartment buildings. Wearily, they sat down on the curb.

Suddenly, in the midst of their meal, they heard a sharp cry. "Look out! Get out of the way!"

A small truck hurtled up the alley from the beach with its lights out. The boys and girls scattered like tenpins, and their food wound up splattered all over the front of the truck. Seconds later, the vehicle plunged out the other end of the alley and turned onto a relatively quiet street that had not attracted the crowds.

"Who in the world was that?" Bess cried. "Look at my blouse! I'm covered with pizza."

"We're all full of food," George grumbled. "On the outside, I mean."

Nancy was on her feet, staring up and down the alley. "Who gave us that warning shout?" she wondered.

Suddenly, a tall man with his hat pulled low over his face appeared at the head of the alley. Nancy wheeled and looked toward the other end. Two more men were approaching from that direction! In the dim light, she could not tell anything except that they seemed strong and walked very purposefully.

A cold shiver ran down the girl's spine.

"We're trapped!" she hissed.

14

Hidden Talkers

The young people stared back and forth from one end of the alley to the other as the menacing figures moved in closer.

Ned quickly took charge. "Nancy, Bess, George. Over here, quickly, against this wall. Burt, you and Dave take those two." He indicated the men closing in from the east. "I'll tackle the other one."

"Wait a minute," Nancy objected. "We don't even know who they are."

"That's true," Ned agreed. "But we should be ready for anything."

"Right," Nancy said. "However, let's try peace talk first."

She stepped up next to Ned. "Hello," she said to the stranger who had now reached them.

"If you had gotten here a few minutes earlier, we could have offered you some food. But now it's all gone because of that truck. Did you see him tear through here?"

There was a moment of tense silence as the man shoved his hat out of his face. Then came the drawling, familiar voice of Albert, their bodyguard. "We saw him, all right. That's why I shouted."

"Oh-h-h!" Bess exclaimed in relief. "Albert, you scared us almost as much as the truck, but I'm glad you did!"

"Yes," Dave added. "And here we were getting ready to take you out with an end sweep!" He referred to one of the especially successful plays the boys had run as members of the Emerson College football team.

Ned gave Dave a playful shove. "If we had tried that on Albert and his friends here, we'd all wake up tomorrow and our first words would be 'Good morning, nurse.'"

Everyone laughed, then Albert said, "I don't want to alarm you, but there are at least four or five suspicious-looking characters who have stayed fairly close to you."

Nancy gasped. "Are you sure?"

"Yes. But I have a feeling all they're trying to

110

do is scare you. Like this. Excuse me, Miss Drew, but would you turn around so that your back is in the light?"

Nancy was puzzled but did as Albert asked. When George saw her back, she gasped.

"What is it?" the titian-haired detective inquired anxiously, then she felt something being pulled off her T-shirt. She whirled around and saw that Albert was holding a six-inch-square piece of cloth with a shiny adhesive back. It was the dreaded omen of the Brotherhood of the Vulture!

Nancy was angry that someone had dared to stick the decal on her clothes. "It must have happened when we bought our food," she said. "If it had been on my shirt longer than that, someone would have noticed it."

"Well," Albert said, "don't worry. We'll be around in case the gang's trying to play tough."

"Does that mean we can't split up?" Ned asked.

"No," Albert said. "You can go your separate ways, but always in pairs. This way we three can keep you covered."

"Good," George spoke up. "Then I vote that we go over to that ice cream parlor we saw about a block up the road."

"I'll buy that," Burt agreed.

"You heard him," cried Dave. "He said he'll buy. What a nice guy."

Laughing, Burt, Dave, Bess, and George started for the ice cream parlor but Nancy held back. Ned nodded knowingly. "Yes," he said, almost reading her mind, "Good idea. I would like to find out more of what's going on with these bodyguards and people following us."

They walked away from the crowds in a northerly direction, glancing back casually every once in a while.

"I think we have a shadow," Ned said suddenly. "This guy's been with us for two blocks."

"Let's go around the corner and see if we can shake him," Nancy suggested.

Quickly, the two changed direction. They noticed a dimly lit restaurant to their right. "In there!" Nancy said and pulled Ned inside. They slipped all the way to the last booth, then watched the entrance to see if the man would follow. A few moments later, someone did come into the restaurant, but the young detectives recognized him as Albert, their protector.

"That's definitely not whom we saw before," Nancy whispered.

Ned nodded. "You know, it's strange that nobody is in this place. With all these people on the beach—"

Nancy giggled. "Maybe the food's no good. You see—" She interrupted herself when voices drifted through the thin partition that separated them from a room in the back. The very first words made her eyes pop open. She signaled frantically to Ned not to speak. Someone had mentioned Penny Black, the rarest and most expensive stamp in the world! The same stamp that had been found in Argentina and was then stolen by Stroessner's gang!

Nancy and Ned listened attentively, but only small snatches of the conversation came through the wall, even though they put their ears directly against it.

"The machines will be ready today, Bigley—"

"Got to get the other big ones . . ."

"We know they're there. Hit 'em tomorrow night."

Nancy's mind began piecing the words together, disconnected though they were. Machines. That could refer to the counterfeiting equipment that Carson Drew and Señor Segovia were trying to find. But, "the other big ones"? What could that mean? More machines? Or other stamps? "We know they're there," and "Hit 'em tomorrow night." Did that refer to a planned theft? Or could it mean a shipment was being brought into Florida?

If only she could find out who was talking behind that wall! Wanting to communicate with Ned but hardly daring to breathe for fear the crooks on the other side would hear her, Nancy looked for something to write on. She rummaged in her bag, but found her note pad and pencil gone, along with her wallet! She motioned to Ned that her purse had been picked, then gestured to ask if he had paper and pencil. He shook his head.

Nancy took Ned's hand into hers, and tapped out a message in Morse code.

These are the men who steal stamps, she signaled.

Ned nodded.

Got to go out back.

Ned nodded again.

Nancy was about to stand up, when a word came from behind the partition that electrified her. A man whose voice appeared vaguely familiar addressed his partner as Otto! And Otto was Stroessner's first name!

She felt her blood surge as suddenly someone started yelling at them. "What are you doing here? You're not supposed to sit back here!" The speaker was a thickset man with greasy hair, who wore a tuxedo. Nancy thought he looked like a movie gangster.

At the same time, cries of consternation issued from behind the wall. Chairs scraped back. Obviously, Otto and his friend had heard the noise and realized that someone had been sitting next to the dividing wall.

"Didn't you see the sign?" the unpleasant man in the tuxedo shouted. "This restaurant is closed! And you come in anyway and sit in the back where nobody can see you."

Ned's blood pressure began to rise. "Now just a minute, sir. The door was open when we came in. We wanted some privacy so—"

"Never mind, never mind," the man grumbled, waving his arms. "The restaurant's closed. We're not serving anybody."

Nancy heard the sound of feet moving rapidly in the back room. Then an outside door slammed. Stroessner and his friend were getting away!

"Excuse us, please," she said. "We're sorry, and we'll go. Come on, Ned." She started to pull him by one arm, but he was now face to face with the tuxedo man and he wanted to settle the matter before leaving.

"No wonder your restaurant isn't more popular," Ned said angrily, "if this is the way you treat your patrons!"

Out of the corner of her eye, Nancy could see Albert quietly get to his feet and advance toward them.

"Ned!" she urged. "It's not worth fighting about. Let's go. We have better things to do. Remember?"

She emphasized every word to break through the cloud of anger that was getting in the way of Ned's reasoning.

"Oh, right," he said. "I'm sorry."

But as he and Nancy started to leave, a light flickered in the hoodlum's eye. "Just a minute," he said, blocking their path with his bulky body. "You're in a terrible hurry to leave all of a sudden. What's going on here? Did you steal something?"

Nancy heard a car starting up in the driveway next to the restaurant. She decided that Ned and Albert could easily take care of "Tuxedo," so she simply ducked under the hoodlum's outstretched arm and ran for the door. Then she heard a crash and winced. No doubt Albert, Ned, and the unpleasant man had all collided. She could tell from the sound of bodies smashing against furniture, but she had no time to turn around and watch what was happening.

She bolted through the door and ran to the sidewalk just as a black sedan came out of the driveway and turned onto the street. Luck was with her. She got a clear view of the license number, though the faces of the two men in the front seat were obscured by the darkness. Nancy paused a moment to memorize the number, then ran back into the restaurant. The struggle between Albert and Ned on the one side and Tuxedo and a short, ugly fellow on the other was just ending.

Nancy found that her friends had done extremely well. Each was sitting on one of the two subdued restaurant men.

"What should we do with them?" Ned asked.

Before Albert had a chance to comment, Nancy said, "Let them go. But we'll tell the police about them."

Reluctantly, Ned released his hold on Tuxedo while Albert allowed the short, ugly man to sit up. Tuxedo got to his feet painfully and started for the back of the restaurant. Then he turned and shook his finger menacingly at Nancy. "You haven't heard the end of this, Nancy Drew."

Ned grinned at Nancy. "Really, you have some pretty terrible friends. I didn't know he knew you. I guess somebody has spread the word about Nancy Drew through the entire criminal community in south Florida."

"Apparently," Nancy said. "But much as I hate to tear us away from such charming company, I think we'd better go find the others and see what thrilling adventures they've had in the meantime."

Ned nodded. Then he turned to Albert and stuck out his hand. "I want to thank you," he said. "You really know how to handle trouble like this. When you fell in the beginning, I thought for sure you were hurt. But you acted like a Hollywood stuntman and jumped right up again."

Albert laughed. "Pretty good, wasn't it? I *was* a stuntman in films for many years. But my bones got too old for that, day in and day out. As a bodyguard, I don't have to work this hard more than once or twice a year."

The three left the restaurant, Albert again walking some distance behind Nancy and Ned. But the situation had now changed. He had become a friend and they regarded him as one of their crowd.

They went back toward the ice cream parlor where their friends had gone. When they arrived, they saw a long line of people winding out the door.

"Nancy! Ned!" came a voice from the head of the line.

"It's Bess," Nancy said.

Bess, George, Dave, and Burt had obviously been standing in line since the friends had parted. Bess pantomimed thirst, and Nancy indicated that she and Ned would like sodas.

Within a few minutes, the group was together again, thirstily drinking their sodas. "Oh," George said, sighing with relief, "It never tasted so marvelous."

"Yes," Burt added. "There's nothing like standing in line for a week to whet your appetite for a common, ordinary old soda."

Later, they wandered back along the road leading to Señor Segovia's house, breaking into song as they walked, entranced by the silver moon that made the street lights appear pale.

By the time they reached the mansion, their voices were worn out and everyone was yawning. The boys, in particular, were aching and tired after their experience with the Land Rover and their early morning flight. They parted company and went to their rooms.

As Nancy stood in the moonlight that flooded her balcony, she breathed deeply. I'd better get some sleep, she thought, because when I spend the night at Mrs. Palmer's, I certainly won't get any there!

15

Dave Versus Angus

The next morning, the teenagers tumbled out for breakfast shortly after nine o'clock. Mr. Drew and Señor Segovia were already at the table, and Nancy recounted the adventures of the preceding night.

She told them what she and Ned had overheard through the restaurant partition, the mention of Penny Black, and the puzzling order to "hit 'em tomorrow night."

Señor Segovia's brow wrinkled as he tried to make sense of the matter. "I find it hard to believe that Stroessner would be meeting someone in the back room of a restaurant," he said. "On the other hand, who in the world would possibly be discussing the Penny Black in such an atmosphere, *except* Stroessner?"

"Maybe," Nancy suggested, "the person with whom Stroessner was meeting was very nervous and wouldn't risk seeing him anywhere else."

Carson Drew nodded. "As a matter of fact, it was the perfect place," he observed. "The only problem is that your friend in the tuxedo made the mistake of not locking the door, not dreaming that you two of all people wouldn't see his "Closed" sign and walk in."

"I think you're right, Dad. Now, Señor Segovia, can you check out this license plate number?" Nancy quickly wrote it on a paper napkin and handed it to him across the table.

He nodded. "Sure. If the computers aren't down, and these days they seem to be down quite a lot, we should have the answer in a couple of hours."

Pushing their chairs back, Carson Drew and their host excused themselves and wished the young people a full and sunny day.

"Thank you," Ned said. Then he turned to his friends. "Tennis, anyone?"

"How about everybody in the pool?" George suggested.

"Three-man volleyball wouldn't be bad except after a half hour of that in the sun, we'd be tripping over our tongues." Bess giggled.

"Wait," Nancy said. "I have to make a phone call. You all figure out what you want to do and I'll go along with it when I come back."

"Oh, you're not neglecting me again because of business!" Ned cried out, pretending to pout and look sullen.

"She'll be back soon," Burt said and punched his friend playfully in the shoulder. "You can live until then!"

Nancy flashed a bright smile and ran off, her titian hair bobbing. She went to her room and called Mrs. Palmer, asking if the house could be cleared of everyone that evening so that Nancy could lie in wait for the burglars.

"What makes you think they'll strike tonight?" Mrs. Palmer asked.

"I just hope that with no guards on duty and everyone out of the house, they won't be able to resist."

"All right," the old woman said. "Now what'll I have to do?"

"First," Nancy said, "find an excuse for getting Susan and the servants out of the house. I assume the maid as well as the gardener are back today?"

"That's right," Mrs. Palmer said. "And where do you suggest I send them?"

"Oh, Mrs. Palmer, I'll bet you can think of a dozen places. Your maid, perhaps, could visit a relative if you give her a few days off. The gardener—"

"Yes," Mrs. Palmer interrupted, "do tell me what to do with a shy, nervous, old man of seventy-five who thinks it's a big adventure to walk around the block!"

Nancy giggled. "How about sending him to a flower show?"

"What flower show?" Mrs. Palmer cried.

"I don't know. But there's always a flower show."

"Really. Well, I don't know. I'll do my best. But I think it's a lot of nonsense. Why not leave the servants alone?"

"I think we'll leave Errol alone," Nancy relented. "He's been there for one burglary already, and we both trust him, so let him stay. But don't tell him what the plans are and that I'm hiding upstairs."

"What?"

"Don't tell him. The fewer people who know a secret, the better chance of keeping the secret."

"True," Mrs. Palmer said. "I've always said that. I'm glad to hear you start quoting me." She laughed, and Nancy could tell that the old lady was beginning to enjoy the intrigue and excitement of the mystery.

"One more thing," Nancy added. "Is there any way of entering your house except through the front door?"

"Of course there is. It's a big house. There's a door in the back and all the servants have doors leading out from their rooms."

"Fine," Nancy said. "Now do me a favor. One hour before you are ready to leave, have Susan McAfee put the clothes she's going to wear tonight in a suitcase. Señor Segovia's chauffeur will pick it up. By that time, the servants should have left and you should find some pretense for keeping Errol busy in back so that he won't see me come through the front door."

"Nancy, are you out of your mind?"

"I have an idea. Just trust me. And tell Susan she'll get the clothes back in good shape to wear tonight."

Next, Nancy dialed the Fort Lauderdale police, and told them of her plan. She said she would appreciate it if the patrol cars in the area would stay on alert, but not come too close to the Palmer house. "If the burglars show up, I don't want them frightened away by police," the girl added.

She was promised cooperation, and, finished with her work, scampered upstairs to change into a peach-colored bathing suit. Then she ran out to the pool and joined in the fun. After much swimming, diving, and a few impromptu water fights, the six young people stretched out on the grass and admired the fifty-five-foot yacht named *The Segovia*.

"It's some boat," Burt said. "I hope we get to take her out again before we leave."

Suddenly, a cry floated across the water. "Ahoy, *The Segovia!*"

The young people got up and stared at a white and gold boat that came closer and closer and finally pulled up within a hundred feet of them.

"Ahoy!" Bess called out, getting into the spirit of sailing. She raised her hand in a wave.

"Ahoy?" Dave asked. "Since when do you say that, and to strangers yet!"

"It's the law of the sea," Bess replied with a laugh. "You're supposed to say 'Ahoy' when another ship greets you."

"But we're not on a ship."

"Now, now," Ned teased, "let the lady say 'Ahoy,' to this handsome young man who's waving to her."

Dave reddened and grinned.

"Ahoy, *Segovia,*" the voice came again. "This is the good ship *The Flying Scot.* And I'm Angus Campbell, your neighbor across the way." He pointed to another large estate, a half mile down the canal. "The big gray house," he added.

Ned stood up. "Hello, Angus," he called. "We're glad to meet you. We're from River Heights and are down here for the spring holiday."

By this time, the boat had nosed into the dock and the boys helped two crewmen from *The Flying Scot* make it fast.

There were handshakes all around as the tall, smiling, red-headed master of the ship met the others. Nancy looked at him with interest, not simply because he was a handsome young man, but because some sixth sense heightened by her detective training told her there was something unusual about Angus Campbell. She couldn't put it into words, but it was a feeling of danger that was at once attractive and frightening. It didn't really make sense, since there was nothing in Angus Campbell's face to reflect this. He was rather handsome, open, and honest-looking, but his deepset blue eyes gave Nancy an eerie feeling.

"So you're here for the beach parties and the

fun and games," Angus said and turned to Bess as the maid brought him a chair and handed him a tall orange drink.

"That's right," Bess replied and smiled prettily.

"It's a great place," Angus said. "We used to live in the West, until I came here on my spring break two years ago. I wound up staying. My father is an industrialist, or was. He decided to retire and bought that house. We just love it."

"Do you still go to college?" Nancy asked him.

"No. I just loaf and take care of my father's boats and cars." He continued to look with great interest at Bess. This was not lost on Dave, who walked around the edge of the group.

"I understand your father, Carson Drew, is here," Angus now addressed Nancy.

"Why, yes. How did you know?"

"The neighborhood grapevine," the young man replied, "has it that he and Señor Segovia are chasing a bunch of thieves. I hope they're making progress?"

"I really don't know," Nancy said. She had trained herself not to discuss her father's business, or her own, with anyone. "I swim and he works, poor man."

"I understand," Angus went on, "that the Brotherhood of the Vulture is involved in this thievery and smuggling."

"How did you know that?" Nancy asked. She was beginning to wonder why this young man was so inquisitive.

"Easy," Angus said. "Their symbol is pasted onto the side of Señor Segovia's dock!"

"What?" Nancy gasped, and everyone rushed to the edge of the dock to peer over. There, indeed, was the buzzard decal!

"How could that have gotten there?" Bess wailed.

"Fairly easy," Angus replied. "Someone could have sailed past, stopped for a moment, and stuck it on."

"But Señor Segovia has a twenty-four-hour guard," Nancy pointed out. "It would be pretty difficult."

"Nevertheless," Angus said, "it was done." He lounged carelessly in his chair, adjusting the crease in his expensive slacks. "Someone did it. And he is giving you a very definite warning."

"Possibly," Nancy said coolly. "Perhaps those people think that Señor Segovia and my father will be frightened by it. But it won't work."

"Well," Angus suggested, "I would be very careful, anyway. They're bad people to fool with. But say!" He got to his feet and spread his arms in a welcoming gesture. "Why don't you all be my guests for lunch on *The Flying Scot* and come for a sail?"

The six friends looked from one to another.

"That would be scrumptious!" Bess squealed. "Your boat is so beautiful."

"I don't know," Dave objected. "I think Consuelo's already preparing lunch here."

"At ten o'clock?" Angus laughed. "I'm sure she hasn't started yet and her staff would love the rest. Come on with me. We'll sail out into the open sea for a while, fish a bit if you like, talk, dance, and have some cool drinks. Later— lunch."

Dave's reluctance was easily overcome since both Ned and Burt were eager to go. So was George. Nancy cast the crucial vote in favor of accepting Angus's invitation, not so much because of the ride, but because she wanted to find out more about Angus Campbell.

His questions earlier had struck her the wrong way. Also, the young man seemed too purposeful and intelligent to be just a loafer, as he called himself.

Another thing that bothered her was that the

129

two crewmen who actually sailed the ship were rather hard-looking people, and not the least bit friendly to the group. Apparently, neither of them knew English, because Angus talked to them in French. Why would the Campbells hire a crew that didn't speak their language?

As the young people cruised down the Intracoastal Waterway toward the dock area known as Port Everglades, Campbell's Chinese cook and galley man brought his guests sodas. Tapes were played to provide dance music, and the River Heights vacationers scampered all over the boat, admiring the expensive fixtures and the beautiful staterooms that looked as if they belonged on an ocean liner.

Only Dave stood silently, sipping his Coke and watching a laughing Bess dance with Angus Campbell. Ned came up beside him and talked mischievously into Dave's ear.

"Boy, this is a floating palace, isn't it? Just fabulous."

"I know. It's wonderful," Dave grumbled. "What do you want me to do, jump with joy?"

"No." Ned grinned. "I was just thinking, here's this handsome Scottish devil with a big home, a gorgeous yacht, all this money. A personable guy, too. Well-educated, pleasant. What could he possibly want?"

Dave's eyes followed Angus and Bess, who were gliding gracefully around the floor in a slow dance.

"Could we talk about something else?" he said uncomfortably.

"Sure, sure. But I had this idea. There's something Angus needs. And perhaps we should help him get it."

"What's that?" Dave cried, exasperated. He became angrier and angrier as he realized that both Angus and Bess were enjoying themselves immensely.

Ned looked innocently at Dave. "What Angus needs is a steady girlfriend. A girl all his own whom he really likes!"

It took a moment for Ned's teasing to sink in and by the time it had, he had disappeared and was looking down on Dave from the deck above.

"And here I thought you were my friend!" Dave called up to him, starting to smile in spite of himself. "It's a good thing you left, or there would have been a man overboard!"

16

Betrayed!

As the young people enjoyed themselves, Nancy was taking every available opportunity to look over *The Flying Scot*, seeking a clue to the mystery she felt in the personality of Angus Campbell. She noticed, however, that wherever she went, a crewman always seemed to be in view, pretending not to watch her. Yet Nancy's instinct told her that he was doing just that.

At last, she disappeared into the one place he could not follow her—the ornate master bathroom. Closing the door behind her and locking it, she surveyed the room decorated in marble and gold, and as large as her bedroom at home.

After an exhaustive search, she found nothing. She glanced down idly at the magazine rack next to the tub and began leafing through the periodicals. Suddenly, she stopped when she saw a newspaper from a Caribbean country. It was only four days old. She noticed that the rest of the magazines were in English. The Spanish newspaper, torn and crumpled, was the only foreign language publication in view.

Nancy scanned the front page, using her rudimentary knowledge of Spanish to piece together the main aspects of the stories. A mayor had been arrested for fraud. There had been a parade the previous day. At the bottom of the first page, she found what she was looking for—a short story about how a valuable stamp collection had been stolen from the home of a symphony conductor.

Putting the paper under her arm, Nancy exited from the bathroom in time to see the crewman whirl about and begin sweeping. He had obviously grown nervous at the length of time the young detective had been out of his sight.

Walking past him, she smiled. *"¿Habla español?"* she asked, meaning, "Do you speak Spanish?" The man simply stared at her. Nancy tried again, in French. *"Parlez-vous espagnol?"*

The man smiled faintly and shook his head. *"Non, mademoiselle."*

"*Merci.*" Nancy swept past him and out to the fantail where the group of young people was gathered. She saw Bess talking with Angus and realized Dave's anguish. Catching Bess's eye, she made motions toward Dave and then pointed at herself and Angus. Bess smiled and nodded imperceptibly. A moment later, she excused herself and walked over to Dave, dragging the suddenly happy young man onto the dance floor.

Nancy slid into the chair next to their host.

"Well, Angus," she said, "you have a very beautiful ship here. I can't thank you enough for inviting us."

"My pleasure." Angus smiled.

Skillfully, Nancy led the conversation around to college, to his education, and to foreign languages. He told her French was the only language he spoke besides English.

"And your crew only understands French?" Nancy asked.

"That's right. Except for the galley man, of course. He speaks Chinese."

"Hm," Nancy said. "I found this Latin American newspaper and started to read it, but my Spanish isn't good enough. I was hoping someone could help me with an article on the front page that sounds interesting."

She put the paper on the table between them and watched his reaction. There was none.

"I have no idea who left it here," Angus said pleasantly. "But then, I have lots of guests. Several of them speak Spanish, so I couldn't tell you who brought the paper."

"Well," Nancy said, "it's not that important. Have you been sailing in the Caribbean lately?"

"No," Angus said. *The Flying Scot* hasn't been out in a week."

Bess and Dave had walked up and overheard the conversation.

"That's strange," Dave said. "We didn't see her at your dock yesterday. And we have a good view of the canal."

"Oh," Angus said, seeming a bit befuddled. "Yes, that's right. Dad sent her up to Jacksonville for a few days for refitting."

Nancy felt he was lying. If the yacht had been in Jacksonville, where had the four-day-old Latin American newspaper come from? Angus apparently had not looked at the date, and now appeared at ease with his excuse. He's a cool customer, Nancy thought.

But rather than make him aware of her doubts, she turned the conversation in another direction, and they all had a marvelous time as they cruised and feasted for several hours before returning to the Segovia dock. When Nancy finally shook hands with Angus, however, she could tell from the look in his eyes that he was aware of her suspicion.

She hurried to tell her father and Señor Segovia about their encounter, only to find that both men were in the city and would be detained until late that evening.

"What's next on the agenda?" Bess asked when they all sat down on the porch to discuss plans.

"Fun for the rest of the afternoon, work tonight," Nancy said.

"What kind of work?" George asked.

"Well, I'm afraid it's something I have to do all by myself," Nancy replied. "I'm going to stake out the Palmer house!"

"What!" Bess and George chorused.

"Why do you want to go by yourself?" Ned asked. "You have plenty of help around. Why put yourself into such danger?"

"I'm sure the thieves watch the place to make certain no one is home," Nancy said. "I have a plan to get into the house unnoticed, but there's no way to get *you* inside. But don't worry, I alerted the police and I'll call them as soon as the burglars arrive."

At seven-thirty P.M., the Segovia limousine

136

drew up at the Palmer house, and the figure of Susan McAfee alighted and walked quickly up the front steps. The door opened for her, and it wasn't until she was inside that Mrs. Palmer gave a little cry of surprise.

"My goodness!" the woman exclaimed as she stared at the girl before her. With a wig and dressed in Susan's clothes, stood Nancy Drew!

"Shh!" Nancy whispered. "Let me go right upstairs so Errol doesn't see me."

"Don't worry about him. I have him polishing everything in the back."

"Good. Will you pick up Susan's stuff in about ten minutes and return it to her? Also, please tell her to leave through the front door when she's ready to go out."

"Right."

Nancy scampered upstairs with her suitcase and entered the bedroom Mrs. Palmer had set aside for her. Hastily, she changed into her own clothes and turned Susan's things over to Mrs. Palmer.

"Very clever," the woman admitted. "If anyone was watching, they simply saw Susan arrive. And when we both leave, the house will officially be empty. But Nancy, I'm worried about you. You can't tackle the burglars all by yourself!"

"I won't," Nancy promised. "I alerted the

police and I'll call them as soon as someone enters the house. The thieves won't even know I'm here. There are phones upstairs, and that's where I'll stay."

"Good," Mrs. Palmer said. "I hope it works."

A half-hour later, Nancy watched out the window as her limousine took Mrs. Palmer and Miss McAfee away. She was now alone in the house. She checked the telephone in her bedroom to be sure it was in working order. Then she sat down to wait, which was the boring part but important. Without the patience to wait, her detective skills would be wasted.

After about two hours, she cautiously opened the bedroom door and tiptoed to the head of the stairs. She lay on her stomach and peered out between the bannister railings so she could see the front door. Then she thought of all the things that could happen and returned to the bedroom to work out an emergency plan in case the burglars trapped her on the second floor.

Opening the window to the roof, she climbed out. She found that by using a series of hand-holds, she could climb the steep mansard slope and make her way over the top onto a flatter part of the roof. She could not get any further than that unless she wanted to rely on a rickety drain spout, but she could see the street from there and call for help. Not quite an escape route, she thought to herself, but better than nothing. Cautiously, she returned to the bedroom and closed the window. Then she crawled to her lookout post at the top of the stairs again.

They may not come through the front door, Nancy thought, but I have a central location at least.

The minutes ticked by and the old house creaked and groaned. But there was no human sound. Then, at about ten o'clock, she heard movement below and saw Errol walk to the front door. He opened it, though there had been no sound of the great door knocker. Two men entered, wearing work clothes. One carried a very large bag.

Nancy knew instantly that these were the burglars and, with a sinking heart, realized that the friendly, dependable Errol was indeed the inside man. She heard him say, "Might as well start in the parlor this time. But please try not to wreck things too badly."

"We wouldn't have to wreck anything," one of the men growled, "if you were bright enough to find out where she keeps them."

"I've tried," Errol said, his voice almost breaking. "I've tried."

The men had passed from view now, into the

parlor. Quickly but silently, Nancy slid to her feet and went back to her room. She picked up the phone and started to dial the police.

However, the line was now dead!

"Oh, no!" Nancy breathed, checking both ends of the cord, one connected to the phone, the other to the jack in the wall. Nothing seemed wrong with it. Quickly, Nancy went into the other bedroom that contained an extension. It was dead, too!

They cut the wire outside, Nancy thought. Probably as a safety measure before they came in.

From downstairs, she was beginning to hear sounds that tore her heart. The burglars were ripping apart the precious old upholstery. What to do? Could she slip into the center hall, get out of the house, and run for help? It was her only chance, and she had to try it.

Down the stairs she crept, her heart in her mouth as the sounds of destruction continued. Lightly, she ran across the open entranceway into the parlor where Errol and the burglars could see her if they were watching. But her luck held and she dashed to the door. She turned the knob and pulled. But the door would not budge!

She turned the knob the other way and

pulled again. Frantically, she checked for possible bolts and locks, but found nothing.

Rrrrrip! The sound from the parlor was more than she could bear. Perhaps she could slip out of a window! She tried the nearest one, then another. But they were stuck tight, as Errol had said they were. The only window that seemed to open was in her bedroom!

She would have to go upstairs and call for help from the roof. But first she had to go past the parlor entrance again. Would her luck hold a second time?

Nancy had only taken a couple of steps when suddenly one of the burglars, his face flushed from his frantic work, loomed in front of her. She stared at him for a moment, then did the only thing she could think of—she screamed.

She made as much noise as she could on the theory that the one thing that makes thieves nervous is a lot of noise. At the same time, she rushed past the startled man and raced up the stairs. The burglar, who had been more surprised than Nancy by their encounter, stood frozen for a couple of seconds, then he shouted, "Nancy Drew's here! Let's get her!"

With that, he started after the young detective. His partner came right on his heels.

Nancy ran into the bedroom, locked the door,

and quickly pushed a dresser in front of it. But she knew it would not take the men long to break in. She had to act fast!

Taking a deep breath, she opened the window and climbed out. She scrambled up the steep mansard slope to the top of the roof as fast as she dared, yelling and screaming for help all the way up.

A passing motorist heard the turmoil and stopped. He jumped out of his car and looked up.

Nancy had by now reached the top of the roof. "Please, sir," she cried out. "Call the police. There are burglars in the house!"

The man stood rooted for a moment.

"Hurry!" Nancy urged. "They're coming after me!"

"Okay," the man shouted. "I'll get help." He leaped into his car and roared off.

As he disappeared around the next corner, Nancy heard the door of the bedroom splinter. Quickly, she climbed to the flatter part of the roof and made her way to the drain pipe. At the same time, she heard the window being thrown open and the voice of one of the burglars as he stepped on the roof.

But then came the sound Nancy had been waiting for. A police siren wailed in the distance! The burglars heard it, too. They quickly made their way back into the house, and ran downstairs. The next moment the front door slammed and they were gone.

Hastily, Nancy retraced her steps to the window, climbed through to the bedroom, then hurried down the stairs. She went into the parlor, which was a wreck, with chairs and sofas ripped open. But she did not stop to survey the damage. Instead, she raced to the kitchen. There she stopped in surprise.

Sitting in a chair, tied up and gagged, was Errol! Nancy stared at him, then removed the gag.

"Oh, Nancy, dear me, thank you. Thank you," the butler murmured. "Will you please untie me, too?"

Nancy stepped back. "I'm sorry, Errol. But I can't!"

"Why not?" the startled man asked.

"Because I saw it all. I know, Errol. And I'm sad that a trusted and valued employee like you could stoop to something like this!"

Errol's face fell. "I thought I deserved more than what I got after a lifetime of service to her," he said. "Well—" His voice trailed off. Then he lifted his eyes pleadingly to Nancy. "Would you mind giving me a glass of water?

The gag dried out my mouth. Please."

Nancy nodded and went to the cupboard. She took out a glass and filled it at the sink.

When she turned to bring it to him, she gasped.

Errol had freed himself from his bonds and now leaped up from his chair. Apparently, his confederates had not tied him securely!

Before Nancy could flee, he was upon her. The glass tumbled out of her hand as he pushed her against the sink. "It was your misfortune to get in my way, Miss Drew. But you see, it's not too late for me," the butler hissed. "Obviously, I can't let you tell the police, can I?" With that, his hands closed tightly around her throat!

17

Hydrofoiled!

Nancy gulped and tried to push him away. Now the sound of the siren was quite loud and the police car was perhaps only two blocks away.

Suddenly, the butler let go of her. He rubbed his hand over his eyes and made a gesture of defeat.

"I can't do it," he mumbled. "I can't hurt you. I can't hurt anyone. It's not my nature. I'm sorry about what they did to Mrs. Palmer's things. But I won't go to prison like an animal."

With that, Errol ran out and disappeared into his room, locking the door behind him before Nancy could stop him. A moment later, she heard the outside door slam. A car started and roared off just before the police pulled up in front.

Nancy ran to the door and threw it open. Two Fort Lauderdale policemen were walking up the steps.

"I'm glad you got here!" she cried. "I'm Nancy Drew and I called you about the burglars."

The shorter of the two officers smiled at her. "I'm Detective Maniello. Miss Drew, were you up on the roof screaming a little while ago?"

"Yes," Nancy replied, "I certainly was. Two men were coming after me. You should see what they've done to Mrs. Palmer's living room."

The policeman sighed. "Another burglary. I knew it. The minute she called us to lift our round-the-clock guard, the thieves were ready."

"That's true," Nancy said. "But now I can give you a very good description of at least one of the burglars, which should certainly help, and I also know that Mrs. Palmer's butler, Errol, is involved with them and let them in."

"That will help a great deal," Detective Maniello confirmed. "But what I'm afraid of is to face Mrs. Palmer before we catch the criminals!"

Nancy smiled. "You won't have to face her right now because she's out."

The officers took notes as Nancy described the crime and the criminals. Then, after thanking her for her thoroughness, they left.

Soon afterward, Susan and Mrs. Palmer arrived and were greeted with hugs by the young detective.

"I'm so glad to see you," Nancy exclaimed.

"Goodness, what a hugger you are," Mrs. Palmer cried. "I take it something has happened?"

"I'm afraid so," Nancy said sheepishly.

"And you didn't catch them?" Mrs. Palmer challenged, a hint of her old fire in her eyes.

"No, but I saw them and I know who tipped them off. If you'll just sit down a minute, I'll explain."

"I told you, I never sit!" Mrs. Palmer said firmly. "Now what happened?" She started to move toward the parlor.

"Oh, please, don't go in there yet!" Nancy begged.

"Don't be childish. I'm no stranger to trouble and I can imagine what hap—" The woman stopped as she saw the ruins of her living room. She was silent for a moment, rocking slightly, which prompted both girls to hold out their arms protectively. But Mrs. Palmer shrugged them off.

"Stop that now! I'm perfectly all right. Do you think I'm going to have a heart attack over some upholstery? I mean, this isn't the Palace of Versailles. Susan, call the upholsterer in the morning. Get all this repaired."

Mrs. Palmer stamped back and forth, anger in her feet as they came down hard on the floor. Then she stopped and pointed her stick at Nancy. "Well," she demanded. "What were they after? And did they get it?"

"I . . . I . . ."

"You don't know."

"Not yet. But I'm much closer. It's just a matter of checking out a few things. When the police pick up the two men, we'll know."

"Oh, bother," said Mrs. Palmer, banging the end of her cane on the floor. "You're starting to sound like a politician, Nancy."

Susan McAfee cleared her throat. "Excuse me, but Nancy's been on the job only two days and nobody expected her to catch the crooks single-handedly. I think she should be congratulated for—"

"Yes, yes, she's done a good job. Forgive me. I'm just upset that all my gorgeous rugs in there were cut up like that."

Nancy saw the glimmer of a tear on the woman's face, but refrained from trying to console her, knowing that the tough old lady would fiercely resist any show of sympathy or softness.

"Now," Mrs. Palmer demanded. "You said you knew who one of them is. Who is it?"

Reluctantly, Nancy broke the news about Errol. As she had expected, this hit Mrs. Palmer harder than anything. White-faced, the woman sat down and didn't say a word for a long time.

Finally, Nancy broke the silence. "I know that you would rather have lost everything than to find that Errol has betrayed you."

Now Mrs. Palmer did break. A tear rolled down her cheek and her voice cracked when she spoke. "Why did he do it? What did I do wrong? You can know somebody all your life and never *really* know him. I thought I was generous. He thought I was stingy. I just don't know, Nancy."

There was another silence, then Mrs. Palmer went on. "You suspected him all along, didn't you? That's why you wanted him here while everyone else was out."

Nancy nodded. "Unfortunately, they were more cautious than I expected. His two confederates cut the phone line before they came in, so I couldn't call the police. By the time I climbed out on the roof and yelled for help, they made their getaway." She explained in detail what happened, then Susan went to make some tea.

"You were very brave, Nancy," Mrs. Palmer said. "I'm grateful for what you did. Without you, those men would have eventually destroyed my home."

They went to the kitchen where Susan poured the tea, then Nancy cleared her throat. "Mrs. Palmer, I know it's annoying to you to hear the same question all over again, but it's the only way to get the information we need. Try and think what it could be the burglars want. Perhaps it's something from so long ago that you've forgotten where you put it. I'm very young but even I have stashed things away so safely that I don't remember where they are. Sometimes I even forget that I hid them at all! I did it with the first piece of good jewelry my dad ever gave me. I hid it because I was afraid I would lose it. And I couldn't find it for a year!"

Mrs. Palmer smiled. "I know," she said. "I do it all the time, too. But I just can't think of what they could be after. I'm drawing a blank."

Just then, someone knocked on the door. Susan went out and admitted Burt and George, who burst into the kitchen excitedly.

"Nancy, we have to talk to you!" George cried. "We tried to call, but your phone is out of order, Mrs. Palmer. Then we contacted the police and found out that the burglars were here, but are gone now, so we came over to tell you what happened."

Nancy smiled and introduced Burt to Mrs. Palmer and Susan, then motioned for her friends to sit down.

"Now, tell us what's up," she said, when everyone was settled around the table and Susan poured tea for the newcomers.

"Well," George said, "we walked down to the beach again tonight. Bess and Dave went off by themselves, and Ned stopped next to a phone booth to tie his sneaker, when a car drove up. A guy jumped out, went into the phone booth, and Ned could hear every word!"

"What did he hear?"

"Nancy, you're not going to believe this. It's fantastic!"

"I'll believe it! Just tell me."

"Ned thinks it was the same guy who sat in the back room of the restaurant the other night," Burt put in. "He called a number and said, 'Hello, Otto.'"

"He was calling Stroessner!" Nancy broke in excitedly.

"That's what Ned thought. Anyway, the guy was all upset. Said something about having this big problem and that he needed money because the deal fell through. Apparently, Otto gave him a job for tonight. The guy repeated the words Otto was saying. A fast boat will be pulling into Port Everglades. He's to meet it and transfer some valuable cargo. How about that?"

"Sounds good," Nancy said. "Did you call Señor Segovia?"

"Yes, but he and your father are out. Ned rented a speedboat and is waiting for you at the Segovia dock. He didn't use the Segovia boat because it's not fast enough. He wanted to have as much power as possible to keep up with those crooks."

"He needs to know if you can come," Burt said. "If you're still busy here, we'll go with him."

"I'll come," the titian-haired detective said, and got up from the table. "Mrs. Palmer, I'll talk to you tomorrow."

"Let me know if you find out more about my burglars," the woman replied. "And Nancy, thanks for what you've done."

On the way to the Segovia mansion, the trio discussed whether Burt and George should go along with Nancy and Ned.

"I'd like to," George said. "I'm dying to find

out what those crooks are going to do!"

"I know," Nancy said. "But I'd rather you stay at the mansion so you can tell Dad and Señor Segovia what's going on as soon as they come back. Where are Bess and Dave?"

"We don't know. We lost them at the beach somewhere," Burt replied.

"That's another reason for you to stay. When they come back and don't find anyone, they'll worry."

A few minutes later, Nancy met Ned at the dock. He was waiting with a sleek, blue and white racer.

"Wow," Nancy said. "This looks like one of those boats that race to the Bahamas and back."

"It is," Ned replied. "It should be able to keep up with anyone."

Carefully, they pulled out onto the Intracoastal Waterway, making sure all their running lights were on and in good working order.

"Ned, did you call the police?" Nancy asked.

"Not yet," Ned said. "But there's a radio on board. We can do it from here."

"I'll do it now," Nancy said. "I'd feel better if I knew they had a harbor patrol craft in the area."

She got on the radio and began calling. But

abnormal static conditions blocked her transmission. All she could hear was a jumble of cracked voices issuing from the speaker.

"Well," Nancy said, "we'll try it again later. Meanwhile, we'd better watch carefully for our man."

"We're almost there," Ned said. "Over there's the spot Otto designated." He cut the engine and turned off the lights. While the boat bobbed gently in the waves, Nancy told Ned what had transpired at the Palmer house. "I have a sore throat from all that screaming I did," she concluded.

Ned had to chuckle even though he realized how dangerous the situation had been. "I wonder what the neighbors thought," he said.

"They probably figured someone had gone mad. But I was really scared. Those two men kept coming after me. Thank goodness that fellow in the car stopped when he heard me and called the police."

"But you still don't know what the crooks were after, do you?"

Nancy shook her head slowly. "All I know is that the Palmer case is bigger than it appears to be."

"What does that mean?"

"I believe those men who keep breaking into that house are looking for something really important."

"Like what?"

"I don't know. I have a crazy hunch, but it's so crazy I don't want to talk about it yet. Hey, look over there!" Nancy said suddenly. "Is that the boat we're after?"

Ned had borrowed a peculiar pair of binoculars from the butler who was in charge of the Segovia special equipment used for crime detection. They made it possible to see more clearly at night. He adjusted them and peered through them intently.

"I'm not sure," he mumbled. "No, I don't think so. That big boat's a hydrofoil. I can't imagine the smuggling boat being a—"

He stopped and stared silently through the glasses. "Nancy, there's a little boat pulling up to it. Maybe it's the gang after all!"

"Let me see," Nancy begged, taking the binoculars. "That's it!" she cried excitedly. "Please call the police again, Ned!"

He nodded and moved to the instrument panel. As he did, his arm accidentally hit a button activating the spotlight and a distress alarm system buzzer!

Suddenly, a bright beam stabbed across the water toward the two boats and a siren filled the night air.

"Oh, no!" Nancy moaned. "Ned, what happened?"

Her friend lunged to turn off the switch. "I hit it by mistake," he said ruefully. "Didn't even know it was there. I'm sorry, Nancy—"

"Never mind, it wasn't your fault," Nancy said. "Look what they're doing!"

Apparently, the crooks had been alerted, because there were some frantic shouts, then a small suitcase was passed from the large boat to the smaller one. The next instant, the small boat sped north up the waterway, its powerful engine snarling loudly.

Nancy shoved the throttle forward and followed. "Ned, try the police again, please!"

Ned grabbed the radio mike. "Fort Lauderdale police," he called. "Attention, please. This is Ned Nickerson and Nancy Drew in Port Everglades Harbor. We're heading north in pursuit of a high-powered boat believed to be carrying contraband goods that are being smuggled into the country."

There was no answer but Ned repeated his message. Meanwhile, the boat they were following gained on them considerably. "We're losing it," Nancy murmured. "It's too fast. They—Ned, it's no use. Look!"

"The little boat's a hydrofoil, too!" Ned said. "Obviously, the gang uses these in all their operations, so they can get away in a hurry if need be. Oh, Nancy, we'll never catch up with them!"

18

A Mystery Solved

Nancy throttled down to normal cruising speed and looked at Ned. He was sitting with his head down. "Boy," he said, "did I mess that up."

Nancy ruffled his hair with one hand. "Nonsense. It was an accident. Anyway, even if you hadn't hit the light and the siren, we couldn't have caught them."

"But if they hadn't known about us, they might have taken off at a slower speed and we might have been able to follow them," Ned said. "Don't try to let me down easy, Nancy. I goofed, and we both know it."

"No sense crying over spilled milk," Nancy said brightly. "Apparently, the radio didn't work, either. Sometimes the breaks are with you, and sometimes they aren't. By the law of averages, we should have luck the next time."

"I'm glad you're an optimist!"

Nancy chuckled. "As Winston Churchill said, I'm an optimist because that means living in hope. If you're a pessimist, you're always living in despair."

"Sounds reasonable," Ned agreed.

When they arrived at the Segovia mansion, he got out to tie up the boat. In the process, his feet got tangled up in a line and he stumbled. The next moment, he crashed headlong onto the dock!

"Oh, no!" he cried. "This isn't my day! Nancy, just take me inside and point me toward my room. Don't let anybody talk to me until tomorrow, or I might accidentally destroy the whole world!"

Nancy was laughing all the way up to the house. Ned went straight to bed as he promised, but she got herself some milk and went out to the patio where Bess, Dave, George, and Burt were anxiously waiting to hear what had happened. Mr. Drew and Señor Segovia had not returned yet.

The foursome was surprised when Nancy told about their adventure, and Burt laughed about Ned's misfortune. "We were wondering why he disappeared so quickly without even saying good night," the boy said. "He probably figured we'd give him the Dummy of the Day Award."

"It wasn't his fault." Nancy defended her friend, but she couldn't suppress a smile.

Next morning when Nancy came down to breakfast, her friends were already sitting there with Mr. Drew and their host. The men had returned late the night before and were now eagerly listening to the young people's account of the latest events.

"The whole thing was really my fault," Señor Segovia said. "If we had left word where to reach us, we would have gotten the police and helped you. But we were moving so fast that we didn't think of it."

"Then you're not angry with us?" Nancy asked.

Señor Segovia laughed. "Angry with you? Never. Your Uncle Ricardo can never be angry with you, Nancy. There. I've made you an honorary niece."

"Can you really do that?" Ned asked him kiddingly.

"Sure," Señor Segovia replied. "I have full permission. Oh, there is a good story I must tell you. Robert Louis Stevenson, the famous novelist who wrote *Treasure Island* and *Kidnapped*, once got a letter from a little girl who complained that her birthday was on Christmas.

Since the Lord's birthday was the big event, people seemed to forget hers and didn't realize that this made her very unhappy. So you know what Stevenson did? He wrote the little girl a letter, officially giving her *his* birthday to be her very own, forever, so that she could have a normal celebration just like other children."

"Hey, that's really neat," Nancy said. "I love that story and I love being your adopted niece, Uncle Ricardo."

Señor Segovia laughed, delighted. Then his expression changed and he held up one finger. "Oh," he said, "I almost forgot. We have some information on that license number you gave me. Let's see. I have it right here." He dug a piece of paper from his pocket. "Does the name Errol Bigley mean anything to you?"

Nancy stared at Señor Segovia and began to nod her head. "Yes, yes. It does," she said excitedly. "I'll bet Bigley is the last name of Mrs. Palmer's butler Errol, the man who is involved with the burglars that wrecked her house. Why don't I call her and confirm this?"

Without waiting for an answer, she ran into the house, and appeared a few minutes later with a triumphant smile on her face. "Bigley is our Errol all right," she said. "Not only that, but something just clicked in my brain!"

"What's that?" Ned asked, curious.

"When we were in that restaurant and overheard the men in the back room talking, one of the voices seemed vaguely familiar to me. But I couldn't place it. That's because I didn't connect Errol with Stroessner's people then. Otto addressed him as Bigley, so no doubt it was Errol!"

"Wow!" Bess and George said almost simultaneously. "What a revelation!"

"Very good, Nancy," her father said proudly. "But now comes the big question. What were they looking for in Mrs. Palmer's house? She never collected stamps. I know that for a fact."

"Oh." Nancy's face fell. "Are you sure?"

"Positive. My ears are still burning from a fifteen-minute lecture she gave me when I was about twenty years old. She said an active young man shouldn't waste his time sitting around sorting little pieces of paper."

"Aw, what a break," Nancy said. "But then, what *were* they looking for?"

No one had an answer.

"I'm going to see Mrs. Palmer right after breakfast," Nancy decided. "If only she could tell us what's hidden in her house. We're getting so close!"

"We're getting close, too," Señor Segovia

said. "I think we've found Stroessner's headquarters."

Before he could explain further, a phone call forced him and Mr. Drew to leave immediately.

"Do you want us to go to Mrs. Palmer's with you?" George asked Nancy.

"No, that won't be necessary. I have a job for you, however."

Dave pretended not to be pleased. "Come now, Nancy. Work again? I was looking forward to a swim!"

"You'll get that while you're working," Nancy replied.

"How?"

"I want you all to watch Angus's place. The butler will give you the proper binoculars. Have fun around the pool but always keep an eye on the canal, okay?"

"That's the kind of job I like," Dave said. "Thanks, Nancy."

Ned said, "I'll come with you to Mrs. Palmer's. There'll be enough watchers here."

Nancy smiled. "Good. Let's go."

Soon André deposited the couple in front of the Palmer house. "I won't be able to wait for you," he said, "since I have a number of errands to run. Would you mind taking a taxi home?"

"Of course not," Nancy said. "And thanks for bringing us here."

She and Ned walked up to the house, and Susan McAfee led them into the kitchen. Nancy told Mrs. Palmer of Errol's connection with Stroessner and of their first suspicion that what the burglars were after was a stamp collection. But the woman reacted as Carson Drew had predicted.

"Your father's right. I think stamp collecting is so much nonsense. Cultivating a garden or making something, now those are worthwhile hobbies. But collecting little scraps of paper? Ridiculous."

"Well," Nancy said, "then the gang must be looking for something other than stamps. Do you have a safe in the house or a safe-deposit box in the bank?"

"Yes," said Mrs. Palmer. "Both. Let's look here first." She led them to a wall in the living room that contained a fireplace. "Pull out the andirons," she instructed Nancy. The girl did so. "Now," Mrs. Palmer said, "press the third brick from the left in the fourth row from the top."

Nancy complied but nothing happened. She looked questioningly at Mrs. Palmer.

"Patience," the old lady said. "That deactivated a catch on the bottom of the fireplace floor. Push it."

Nancy did as she was told. The slab slowly moved down about four inches and then slid easily to the left. Embedded in the floor, face up, was a very strong-looking safe!

Nancy was filled with admiration for whoever had designed the safety precautions. "That is really well thought out," she said.

"Correct." Mrs. Palmer nodded. "A devious mind came up with that one. Now let me try the combination." Bending down stiffly, the old lady tried to turn the dial. It wouldn't budge. Nancy and Ned worked on it, but to no avail.

"Well," Mrs. Palmer said, "that's what I get for not using the safe more than once every twenty years. I'll have to ask the locksmith to open it. But before I do that, we may as well go to the bank and check the safe-deposit box."

The group drove a short distance to Mrs. Palmer's bank and examined everything in her box—stocks, bonds, deeds, various legal documents, and a great deal of expensive jewelry.

Nancy sighed. "The burglars could've been after any of this," she said. "But I can't help thinking that if they wanted to steal this type of thing, they would have taken some of the valuables in your house, even though they are a bit bulky."

"True," Mrs. Palmer agreed. "Well, let's get the locksmith and go back to the dreary job of opening that safe in the fireplace."

The locksmith, a young and nervous man, was immediately cowed by Mrs. Palmer's gruff, critical manner. As he worked, she stood over him, watching every move. As a result, it took him twice as long as usual. But he finally did hear the last tumbler click and swung the heavy door up.

"It's a very inconvenient position for a safe," he said, stretching his back.

"Of course it's inconvenient," Mrs. Palmer declared. "That's to make sure nothing is put in it frivolously. In a safe like that where you practically crack your back trying to get to it, you only put truly valuable things." She scowled at him and the young man shrugged apologetically.

"Yes, ma'am. I see your point," he said.

"Oh, Land of Goshen, don't be so wishy-washy. Is it convenient or isn't it?"

"Oh, yes," the confused young man said. "Very convenient."

"It is *not!*" Mrs. Palmer snapped. "We've just

settled the fact that it was the most inconvenient safe ever made!"

The young man stared at her, slightly dazed, as if he had just had a narrow brush with a bolt of lightning. "Uh, yes, it's inconvenient, but that's convenient because then you only put important stuff in. Isn't that what you said?"

"You got it. Now get on with you. Your work here is finished."

"Yes, ma'am, thank you."

"You're welcome," Mrs. Palmer said, dismissing him. But the young man stopped and turned back, squaring his shoulders.

"Are you still here?" asked Mrs. Palmer, peevishly.

"Yes, ma'am. I just wanted to ask you a question. Since you only put the most valuable things in that safe, can you remember what you put in it?"

Mrs. Palmer was bent over, peering into the safe. She stopped, then straightened and turned to stare at the young man.

"Can you remember, Mrs. Palmer?" he repeated.

"I heard you," Mrs. Palmer said. "I'm not handicapped. I'm trying to think." She paused, then looked the young man straight in the eye.

"No, I'm not able to remember. And you're a

rascal to challenge me on it. But you're walking out with more backbone than you had when you came in. That's my talent, young man, putting backbone in people. I get 'em mad at me and pretty soon they start acting like real, living, breathing people."

The young man smiled, tipped his cap, and left.

In the meantime, Nancy had been fidgeting and going on tiptoe, waiting for the conversation to end, curious to see what was in the safe.

"Now then," Mrs. Palmer said, "let's see what we have here." She reached inside. The instant her hand came out of the safe, clutching a bundle of old letters, Nancy knew what the thieves had wanted. But to be sure, she waited.

"Well," Mrs. Palmer said, "nobody would be interested in these. They're love letters sent to my grandmother from my grandfather when he was working as an engineer in the jungles of South America."

"But that's it!" Nancy cried. "Don't you see, that's exactly what those crooks are after!"

19

Stroessner's Plan

"What!" Mrs. Palmer cried. "They want my grandfather's letters? What for? Blackmail? My grandparents have been dead for more than fifty years!"

"No, no!" Nancy said excitedly. "Not the letters. The envelopes, or rather the stamps on the envelopes. There must be some particularly valuable ones that they know were purchased in those days. And from the looks of that huge bundle of letters you have, there must be easily a couple of hundred stamps."

"Well, of all the silly—"

"Yes, silly perhaps, Mrs. Palmer. But please, let me check it out. I'd like to show those envelopes to Señor Segovia. He'll have the stamps evaluated and give you some idea of whether they were worth all this trouble to get them."

"I can't believe it. I think those people are mad," Mrs. Palmer declared.

"Money mad," Nancy added.

The woman agreed to remove the letters and give Nancy the envelopes. As she did, Nancy and Ned sorted them by stamps, putting all the unusual ones in one pile and the others, that appeared on many letters, in another. "This will save Señor Segovia some work," Nancy said as she combined the two bundles in the end, and put them in a shopping bag Susan gave her.

Then the young people caught a cab that was parked not far from the Palmer home.

"The driver must have let someone out just a second ago," Nancy said. "Weren't we lucky!"

Somewhat tired after the excitement of their last discovery, they rode in silence for a time until Nancy said, "I don't think the driver has the right address." To be sure, she repeated it. The man nodded but did not turn around. Instead, he continued to drive in the wrong direction.

Ned tapped on the window. "Listen," he said, "you're going the wrong way. You're heading west, taking us inland. We want to go to a house on the canal!"

The man turned his head slightly. "You may

as well settle back and relax. You're going where I've been told to take you. And, by the way, the boss says thanks for finding the stamps."

"What!" Nancy cried, feeling her heart sinking. "What are you talking about?"

"We've got ways of finding out things. We keep a watch on the old lady's place. When she went to the bank and came back with the locksmith, we knew we were on the trail. We knew she was going to dig those letters out. And you have them right now, in that shopping bag. But you won't turn them over to Segovia. The Big Man will get them."

"Stroessner," Ned said, disgusted.

"You said it, I didn't."

"Oh, come on," Ned said. "Everybody knows Stroessner is the crime kingpin."

"Stroessner? Oh yeah, that's the gentleman who is a stamp dealer. The police and Segovia are saying he's the head of some criminal gang? I don't know anything about that." The driver laughed harshly.

Nancy sighed. "That's the way the big ones always protect themselves from justice. They pay you guys to do the dirty work and keep their names out of it."

Ned frowned. "What are we going to do?

Want me to try to break the glass and get at him?"

Nancy shook her head. "There is an easier way and no one will get hurt." She reached into the shopping bag and pulled out an envelope.

Then she tapped on the glass. "Sir. Oh, sir. Could I have your attention a moment?"

"What do you want?" came the irritated response. "I gotta watch the road!"

They came to a stop light and Ned tried opening both doors. They were locked and under the driver's control. So were the windows. They could not be rolled down.

Nancy shook her head. "That won't work. Even if we yell and scream nobody will notice. Let me try my approach." She tapped on the window again.

"Sir," she said, "what would happen to you if you arrived at your headquarters and you told the boss that you had *us* but *didn't* have the stamps?"

"What are you talking about? I got you *and* the stamps," came the sullen reply.

"Oh, no," corrected Nancy. "You have *us*. And *we* have the stamps. But suppose I take the envelopes and as you're driving I tear up *every stamp?*"

Nancy and Ned went crashing against the

front seat as the driver hit the brakes in a panic and then speeded up again. "Now don't go saying things like that," he shouted. "You wanna turn my hair white with worry? You just be good and leave those stamps alone. In fact, I better stop and take them."

"Better not," said Nancy. "I have a lighter here that's full of fluid. I can douse them and set fire to them faster than you can turn around."

The driver hunched his shoulders and wiped his brow. "Wait a minute," he said, slowing down, "let's talk this over."

"Don't slow down," Nancy warned.

He ignored her.

"Okay," the young sleuth cried, "here goes the first one." She tore an envelope right through the center of the stamp.

The driver almost went mad. "Don't do that! Lady, listen! Stop doing that!"

Nancy tore another one.

"All right!" he screamed. "What do you want?"

"Turn us loose in a well-populated area and I'll give you the letters," Nancy said.

"Nancy!" Ned whispered. "You can't do that!"

Nancy nudged him with her foot and he realized that she had a plan. He lapsed into silence and waited to see what would happen next.

"How do you want to handle this?" the driver asked.

"Take us to downtown Fort Lauderdale."

"Nothing doing. The cops'll catch me. Too much traffic."

"Then go to North Federal Highway and Oakland Park Boulevard," Nancy said, naming an intersection in the north of town where there were shopping centers. She knew she and Ned could easily slip away once they left the cab, and the driver would not be afraid because the traffic was not heavy enough to block his escape.

"All right," he agreed.

"What are you doing?" Ned hissed.

"Trust me," Nancy said softly.

When they reached the intersection, she had the driver pull up to the curb.

"Hand me the letters," he demanded, reaching back to unlock the sliding partition.

"Not on your life. I'll set fire to them."

"*No!* Okay. How do you want it?"

"I'll leave the letters on the back seat, see?" She pointed.

"No good," he objected. "You throw them to me before you get out."

"Only if Ned leaves the car first and the door is open."

"Fine." The driver reached back. "Give me your hand."

Nancy hesitated, but then put her hand forward. She felt the man clamp his viselike fingers around her wrist. "Now," he said, "tell your friend to get out."

Ned did and held the door open.

"Throw me the letters," the driver commanded.

With her free hand, Nancy tossed the envelopes over the divide. With the light turning green, the man had no choice but to release her hand since there were cars in back of him. As he did, Nancy leaped out. Ned grabbed her, slammed the taxi door, and they started running toward the shopping center.

The driver took off with his tires squealing, and quickly disappeared into the distance.

"Well!" Ned gasped as they stopped running and hailed another taxi that was parked first in line near a large department store. "We're free, but they have the goodies."

"Only some," Nancy said, reaching into her purse.

"What?"

"When we sorted the stamps, I put the envelopes with special ones on top, and the repeats on the bottom. I took everything out of the shopping bag, but only gave him the bottom pile. The rest I put in my purse."

Ned laughed. "Nancy, you're so clever. The guy never knew you had more envelopes!"

"Right!"

"Stroessner will have his head!"

"Those are the hazards that go with his profession," Nancy said with a chuckle.

When they returned to the mansion, she gave the envelopes to Señor Segovia, who promised to have them checked by an expert immediately.

Then Nancy and Ned got sodas for themselves and went out on the patio. Their friends were lounging in chairs, but the atmosphere was tense, and they kept taking turns looking through two pairs of binoculars.

"What's happening?" Nancy asked.

"We found out that good old Angie's house over there isn't just a simple home for the Campbells," Ned replied. "It appears to be a meeting place for some really mean-looking characters. Here, take a look."

Nancy took the glasses and eagerly scanned the Campbell home and dock area.

The first thing that caused her to jump was

the sight of a small boat docked next to *The Flying Scot*. It looked exactly like the hydrofoil she and Ned had tried to chase!

She asked her friend what he thought. Ned nodded.

"Exactly. If it isn't, it must be a twin. And look at the driveway!"

Nancy focused on the drive circling the main building. A truck stood near the gate and a piece of machinery, covered with tarpaulins, was being loaded. "It's a press of some kind!" the girl exclaimed.

"They already loaded other equipment," Dave said.

"Oh, dear," Nancy cried, "I have a hunch that this is the place Dad and Señor Segovia are looking for! But the gang's moving out. Why?"

"You must have scared Angus when you talked with him on the yacht," Ned suggested. "He probably figured you knew something, perhaps more than you really did."

Nancy bit her lip. "I guess that wasn't too smart. I shouldn't have let on I was suspicious. On the other hand, he certainly wasn't very bright coming over here and asking all those questions."

"I think," Ned said, "he's the kind of guy who feels he has so much charm he can get away with anything. Only this time he overplayed his hand."

"His father must have been furious," Dave put in.

"I doubt that there is a father," Nancy said. "I have a feeling that Angus works alone. Somehow he got roped into the crime ring and made a lot of money, so he bought this house as a meeting place for the gang. The story about his rich dad is just that—a story."

"You mean, you believe that everything is over there?" Ned asked. "The stolen stamps, including the Penny Black, the counterfeiting equipment—and now they're moving it?"

"That's the way it looks. Let's call Dad and Señor Segovia and have them raid the place," Nancy suggested and turned to walk into the house.

"No good," George told her. "They left for Miami two hours ago because they were following up their hottest tip yet. They're closing in on what they believe is Stroessner's headquarters."

"I bet that tip is just another piece of misinformation that Stroessner leaked to them!" Nancy exclaimed. "Maybe he did it to distract everyone's attention from the Campbell place so he'll have time to move his stuff!"

"Why not just call the Fort Lauderdale police?" Bess spoke up.

"Right," Nancy said and rushed for the phone. But it was dead! Quickly, the staff checked all the extensions in the house and found that every one had been disconnected. André, the chauffeur, finally discovered that the outside line had been cut.

Worried, Nancy rushed to the patio and picked up the binoculars. She was angered to see Angus Campbell staring back at her, smiling and waving while he motioned two small cars in the driveway to move up behind the truck. Apparently, the crooks were about ready to take off!

"There's no time left!" Nancy cried. "If we can't get the police, we have to stop them ourselves!"

Just then, Albert appeared on the patio. "I'd like to help with this," he offered.

"Thank you. Can we get a car?"

"Of course."

Without hesitating, he led them to the light blue limousine and the six friends piled in. After saying something to André, he took the wheel and expertly drove out of the driveway, heading straight for the Campbell mansion.

"I hope we make it. I hope we don't make it. I

hope we make it. No, I don't hope we make it—" Bess was crouching on one of the jump seats, eyes closed and all fingers crossed, worrying about what would happen if they confronted the crooks!

20

The Sinking Earth

George had misgivings, too. "What are we going to do when we get to the place, Nancy?" she asked.

"We can't just jump out and start a fight," Burt said. "From what we've seen, we're sorely outnumbered. We really have to give this some thought."

"I'm thinking right now," Nancy told him. "But so far I have no solution. Let's play it by ear."

Bess got more worried by the minute. "Do you have any suggestions, Albert?" she asked anxiously.

"Maybe," the ex-stuntman said. "André is following us in the gray limo. I figured in this situation you can never have too many cars. I'm not sure what we're going to do with them yet, but whatever it is, we may lose one."

"How can you lose a car?" Bess asked. "They're so big, especially these limousines."

"Bess," Dave said, "you're scared. And when you get scared, you don't think straight. Just try to relax. I promise nobody will hurt you."

"Your hero," George whispered into Bess's ear, and the girl blushed.

"One more thing," Albert said. "We have a radio in the back. One of you should try to reach Señor Segovia. Well, here we are!" He braked slightly and they came to a halt about two hundred yards from the Campbell mansion.

"Do you see anything?" Nancy asked.

"They're about to leave," Albert replied tersely. "Would everybody please get into André's car behind me!"

The young people proceeded to do so. Nancy, who climbed out last, looked at him intently. "What are you going to do?" she asked.

"We'll have to buy time until we reach the police. I'll try to block their escape route. You see, they have only one driveway entrance, right there at the gate. The drive loops around the house."

"You're planning to block the entrance?"

"Right. It won't hold them for long, but it

might give us five or ten minutes more time."

"Please be careful!"

The stuntman smiled. "Don't worry, I always am. That's why I have managed to live so long and stay so ugly."

Nancy smiled at Albert's handsome face that was crisscrossed with scars and featured a nose that had been broken several times. "You're not ugly," she said. "Right now, with what you're going to do, you're the most beautiful man in the world!"

Albert laughed and Nancy joined her friends in André's car. They all watched tensely as the stuntman revved up his engine. Then he shot forward.

The big limousine gathered speed until it was traveling about forty miles per hour. At precisely the right moment, Albert turned violently, got up on two wheels, and started to skid sideways. When he came down again, he crashed into the gate!

The young people gasped and waited anxiously. Finally, Albert extricated himself from the driver's side, grinned, and ran toward them.

They heard the strangled cries of surprise and rage as the crooks, who had just begun to move their convoy of two cars and the truck, found themselves halted by the large limousine that was wedged in between the gateposts.

When Albert reached the young people, he asked, "Have you been able to contact Señor Segovia yet?"

"No," Nancy replied. "But we got the police."

"Are they coming?"

"Yes, even though they had a hard time believing this is happening."

"I don't blame them," Bess said. "I can hardly believe it myself, and I saw it with my own eyes!"

Just then, a message came crackling over the radio. The police had gotten in touch with Mr. Drew and Señor Segovia, and the two men were on their way with federal officers.

The six friends cheered, but Albert bit his lip. "They'd better get here soon. See what those crooks are using to get out of that driveway?"

Nancy peered through the foliage. A bright yellow bulldozer was charging toward the gate!

"Bye-bye limousine," Albert said softly. Luckily, he had done such an expert job of wedging the car in, that it took the bulldozer almost five minutes to smash it and push it out of the way. Then the gang came roaring out of the gate. André immediately took up the pursuit.

Nancy broadcasted constant position reports to her father and the police as they followed the gang. Where could the crooks be heading? she wondered. Not to a boat. That would be too slow and they'd be caught. They had to be planning to get away by air. But if that was the case, they wouldn't have time to load the machinery. The best Stroessner could hope for was to escape with the stamps, which would be a victory for him. The stamps were the most valuable part of the criminals' operation and would enable them simply to set business up elsewhere. They could always get new counterfeiting equipment.

André had to use all his driving skills to keep up with the mad gang as the truck and the two cars careened wildly over the highway.

"Maybe I'd better drive," Albert suggested.

"Good idea," André agreed. "I'm not up to the stunts that are required for this job!" He pulled over to the side and quickly let Albert take the wheel.

At times, the criminals veered into the lane of oncoming traffic. But Albert managed to keep up without endangering anyone.

Nancy was still in radio contact with the police. They were now convinced that Stroessner was headed for an airstrip to the northwest, toward the Everglades. By abandoning the machinery, the crooks could take off from there, provided they had managed to have a plane ready.

"With Stroessner's contacts," Ned said, "I'm sure he was able to radio some confederates to provide an aircraft, even though it was very short notice."

The others agreed. Soon they found themselves on a two-lane road, which inspired the crooks to even worse driving. Unfortunately, there was no sign yet of the police.

Finally, because of the risks the gang was taking cutting in and out of traffic, Albert had been forced farther and farther back, with several cars between him and the criminals.

Yet, Nancy and her friends had not given up hope of catching up with the gang, until they saw the outline of a small, twin-engine aircraft in the distance.

"That's it!" George cried. "I bet that's how they'll get away, and we won't be able to do anything about it!"

Albert's lips were pressed tightly together. If only he could diminish the gap between the limousine and the fleeing caravan! But he had no choice but to crawl along behind two slow-moving cars and watch the gang turn off the road. The caravan sent up plumes of dust as it headed for the plane along a dirt lane.

"Oh," Bess moaned, "they're going to make it!"

It certainly appeared that way. The police cars were still a mile away, and the traffic in front of the pursuers continued to stutter and stall.

Then, just as things began to move again and Albert picked up speed, there was a loud explosion!

The limousine swerved violently and he could hardly control the wheel. "Blowout!" he muttered. "Stay calm. It's all right."

He reduced the speed to five miles an hour. Ned and the boys could stand it no longer.

"We're pretty good runners," Ned said. "Let us out and we'll get there faster than you will."

Albert shook his head. "You may be good runners, but what will you do when you catch up to them? The three of you couldn't stop that whole gang, even if they're not armed. The best you could do would be to wave good-bye to them."

"Oh, this is maddening!" George clutched her head in her hands.

Nancy just nodded. As they bumped along, they could see the villains climbing from their vehicles and running toward the plane.

"Now I know why they took the truck, even though they're not planning to unload the equipment," Dave said. "They couldn't all fit into the cars!"

"Where are the police?" Burt said impatiently.

As if in answer, they heard Señor Segovia's voice over the radio. "We're coming, we're coming. We can see the plane in the distance. Let's hope it'll take the gang a few minutes before they fly off."

But the criminals were boarding the plane already, and the pilot revved up the engines. Nancy grew desperate. She took the radio microphone and called the police again. "Is there no way we can get a helicopter here to stop them?" she asked.

"Negative," came the answer. "All copters are on emergency missions and we anticipate it will be another hour before one is available."

"What about a chase plane?" Nancy urged.

"Negative again. Same situation. All police planes are involved in a rescue operation that involves human lives. We can't take any away from that mission."

"Thank you." Discouraged, Nancy put the microphone down. "Well," she said, "that's it.

Stroessner's going to get away by seconds."

Albert had now reached the dirt lane into the field and turned. Slowly, the limousine bumped toward the aircraft. "I'll try to head them off," the ex-stuntman said, and aimed for the end of the runway.

Just then, the pilot started to taxi toward that spot. To the complete surprise of the group, the plane had only gone about fifty yards when its front end dipped and seemed to run into a hole. It dipped again, then the whole plane vanished!

The young people gaped. "What—what happened?" Nancy cried out.

Albert came to an abrupt stop. "We'd better not go any further," he declared tersely. "There seems to be a sinkhole up ahead."

"A what?" Bess asked.

"A sinkhole. That's why you can't see the plane. It sunk." He jumped out of the car. "Any volunteers who want to come with me and see what happened to our friends?"

"Will we sink?" Bess asked warily.

"Not much."

Everyone got out and followed Albert. When they came closer to the area where the plane had disappeared, they realized that the ground had become depressed ten or twelve feet.

"How did this happen?" George inquired.

"These sinkholes are the result of a low water level under the earth," Albert explained. "When the water recedes, it leaves empty space, and sometimes the earth collapses ten or fifteen feet in the center. It's enough to keep an airplane from taking off. But the sides of the hole are usually not steep, so it's not nearly as bad as it looks."

Nancy suddenly smiled. "The crooks, who thought they were so clever, provided for every emergency except an act of nature."

At this moment, a number of police cars came up and stopped near the limousine. Carson Drew, Señor Segovia, and several officers jumped out and ran up to the group.

Nancy hugged her father. "Look, Dad, there are your crooks!" she cried, pointing to the plane, now barely visible.

"Sitting in a sinkhole seems rather fitting for them, doesn't it?" Ned added.

With the police in the lead, the group went to the edge of the hole. They saw a big, bald man with a monocle, obviously Otto Stroessner, perspiring and cursing as he was trying to climb up the side. He clutched a briefcase that everyone was sure contained the rare stamps. Behind him was Angus Campbell and the two

French sailors; the restaurant owner whom Nancy had dubbed "Tuxedo" and his helper; the two burglars that had destroyed Mrs. Palmer's living room; Errol Bigley; and the three men who had kidnapped Mr. Drew. There was also another man whom the young people had never seen before.

"Is that McConnell?" Nancy asked Señor Segovia. He nodded.

Quickly, the police handcuffed the men and led them to the squad cars. As Stroessner went past Nancy, he gave her a furious look.

"I think the Brotherhood of the Vulture is going to lose some of its most valuable members," she said.

He turned red with anger and started to reply, but then restrained himself and walked on. Angus Campbell showed no emotion at all. When he saw Bess, he stopped for a moment. "I'm really sorry we didn't have a chance to get to know each other better," he said with an ironic smile.

Dave kicked some stones. "Don't you ever give up?" he growled. "Even when you're in handcuffs?"

Angus grinned but did not answer.

"Well," Ned said to Dave, "remember what I told you. He probably wouldn't be in this shape today if he had found a nice girl of his own."

"You're a very bad man!" Dave replied, struggling not to chuckle at the kidding.

Nancy stopped Angus. "Tell me," she asked, "why did you suddenly move out all your stuff and leave like this?"

Angus shrugged. "Panic. I realized I had asked too many questions. Also, Stroessner was kind of dumb the way he was flaunting his operation right under the nose of Ricardo Segovia, trying to make a fool of him."

"Shut up!" Tuxedo growled behind him. "Don't say nothing until you see your lawyer, you idiot!"

Angus grinned. "What lawyer? I'll represent myself. You see, I *am* a lawyer, duly admitted to the bar of the state of Florida!"

"I can't stand him," Dave moaned, burying his face in his hands. "Even after he goes to jail, I won't be able to stand him."

Angus shrugged. "Anyway," he said to Nancy, "the clincher was when you found that Spanish newspaper on my yacht. I knew you were suspicious and we were too vulnerable for our own good. If we had been able to relocate without your knowledge, things might have worked out. But—they didn't."

No, they didn't, Nancy thought. She felt satisfaction at having prevented the gang from succeeding, but at the same time, she wondered when she would have another mystery to solve. She had no idea that soon she would be searching for *The Elusive Heiress*.

Later, at police headquarters, Stroessner's briefcase was examined, and Nancy and her friends at last viewed the famous Penny Black stamp. They were disappointed. It was so dark that they could hardly see the outline of the design. It was also slightly dirty.

"That's it?" Bess asked. "And it's worth all that money?"

"That's because it's so rare," Señor Segovia told her. "We also found a number of very valuable stamps on those envelopes that belong to Mrs. Palmer. I already notified her and she said to put them up for auction. The proceeds are to go to her favorite charity."

"Well," Nancy said with a smile, "the sinister omen brought some good after all!"

NANCY DREW® MYSTERY STORIES By Carolyn Keene

THE HARDY BOYS® SERIES By Franklin W. Dixon

POCKET BOOKS PRESENTS MINSTREL BOOKS™

THE FUN BOOKS YOU WILL NOT WANT TO MISS!!

___BASIL OF BAKER STREET Eve Titus 70287/$2.95

___FUDGE Charlotte Towner Graebar 70288/$2.95

___HARVEY'S MARVELOUS MONKEY MYSTERY
    Eth Clifford 70927/$2.95

___MY LIFE WITH THE CHIMPANZEES
    Jane Goodall 66095/$2.75

___HOBIE HANSON, YOU'RE WEIRD
    Jamie Gilson 73752/$2.95

___THE ORDINARY PRINCESS M.M. Kaye 69013/$2.95

___HOW TO PREVENT MONSTER ATTACKS
    David Ross 55832/$2.50

___MONSTER KNOCK KNOCKS
    William Cole & Mike Thaler 70653/$2.75

___HARRIET AND THE CROCODILES
    Martin Waddell 68175/$2.75

___HARRIET AND THE HAUNTED SCHOOL
    Martin Wardell 52215/$2.50

___HELLO, MY NAME IS SCRAMBLED EGGS
    Jamie Gilson 74104/$2.95

___JUDGE BENJAMIN: THE SUPERDOG SURPRISE
    Judith Whitelock McInerney 61283/$2.75

___TALES FROM THE WEIRD ZONE: BOOK ONE
    Jim Razzi 63240/$2.50

___THE NERVE OF ABBEY MARS
    Judith Hollands 70762/$2.75

___SEBASTIAN (SUPER SLEUTH) AND THE
    PURLOINED SIRLOIN
    Mary Blount Christian 63253/$2.50

___HARRIET AND THE ROBOT
    Martin Waddell 66021/$2.50

___WANT TO TRADE TWO BROTHERS FOR A CAT?
    Linda Lewis 66605/$2.75

___WHO'S AFRAID OF HAGGERTY HOUSE?
    Linda Gondosch 67237/$2.75

___NO BEAN SPROUTS, PLEASE!
    Constance Hiser 72325/$2.95

___ADDIE ACROSS THE PRAIRIE
    Laurie Lawlor 70147/$2.75

___HARVEY'S WACKY PARROT ADVENTURE
    Eth Clifford 72908/$2.95

Read On....

___BASIL IN THE WILD WEST Eve Titus 64118/$2.75

___THE DASTARDLY MURDER OF DIRTY PETE
     Eth Clifford 68859/$2.75

___ME, MY GOAT, AND MY SISTER'S WEDDING
     Stella Pevsner 66206/$2.75

___DANGER ON PANTHER PEAK
     Bill Marshall 70271/$2.95

___BOWSER THE BEAUTIFUL
     Judith Hollands 70488/$2.75

___THE MONSTER'S RING
     Bruce Colville 69389/$2.75

___KEVIN CORBETT EATS FLIES
     Patricia Hermes 69183/$2.95

___ROSY COLE'S GREAT AMERICAN GUILT CLUB
     Sheila Greenwald 70864/$2.75

___ROSY'S ROMANCE Sheila Greenwald 70292/$2.75

___WRITE ON, ROSY! Sheila Greenwald 68569/$2.75

___ME AND THE TERRIBLE TWO Ellen Conford 68491/$2.75

___SNOT STEW Bill Wallace 69335/$2.75

___WHO NEEDS A BRATTY BROTHER?
     Linda Gondosh 62777/$2.50

___FERRET IN THE BEDROOM, LIZARDS IN THE FRIDGE
     Bill Wallace 68009/$2.75

___THE CASE OF THE VISITING VAMPIRE
     Drew Stevenson 65732/$2.50

___THE WITCHES OF HOPPER STREET
     Linda Gondosch 72468/$2.95

___HARVEY THE BEER CAN KING Jamie Gilson 67423/$2.50

___ALVIN WEBSTER'S SUREFIRE PLAN FOR SUCCESS
     (AND HOW IT FAILED) Sheila Greenwald 67239/$2.75

___THE KETCHUP SISTERS:
     THE RESCUE OF THE RED-BLOODED LIBRARIAN
     Judith Hollands 66810/$2.75

___THE KETCHUP SISTERS:
     THE SECRET OF THE HAUNTED DOGHOUSE
     Judith Hollands 66812/$2.75